th

by m.gilliland

First published 1986 by Hooligan Press, BM Hurricane, London WC1N 3XX.
This edition published July 1990 by **Attack International**
                              BM 6577
                              London WC1N 3XX
                              England

ISBN 0 9514261 3 3

for a truly free world

one linda

I should have known what he was up to all right but I hadn't a clue. It was easy enough to see what he fancied in her, that Janice was a real beauty. Besides being a stuck up bitch.

Oh yes Janice. She used to have fellas queuing up to go out with her. I suppose we were a bit jealous. But sooner or later she'd tell all of her fellas to fuck off, which only spurred them on more, men bein what they are. There was a whole gang of them down our way had their eye on Janice. Like a pack of randy dogs, sniffing after her hole.

But my Da wasn't one of them. When he took a fancy to Janice he swept her off her feet. You wouldn't believe the nerve of the old bastard, and he married with six kids, of which I was the oldest, being about fifteen at the time. Maybe I loved him so much I was blind to his faults. But this time I couldn't close my eyes.

It all began one day I was walking back to school after the dinner break. It's a big wide road and windy, and it was cold that day. Rubbish and dust blowing. Cars and lorries whizzing by, and the wide road as grey as the sky.

Well, didn't I come by the corner shop, and there was a crowd of girls milling about inside. And there was stuck up Janice herself coming out, and she done up to the nines, and looking down her nose at us convent girls' uniforms. Just cos she worked in a fancy hairdressers. Just at that moment didn't a car pull in out of the traffic. Pulls up. And in hops Janice.

There was girls pushing out past me, and I staring, and I heard someone say - "Hey look at Janice goin off with your Da" - It was. It couldn't be. But it was. I noticed I was going hot all over, but I couldn't stop staring. And just then, as the car pulled away, didn't Janice slip her arm around his shoulder and kiss him on the cheek. She knew well we were watching of course, the sneakin bitch!

Well I'll never forget that moment. The others started nudging and giggling and I hid my face in me long fair hair. Then they started to hoot and jeer me. So I just took to my heels and ran away off down the road.

It's a strange thing but I can trace everything that happened since back to that little kiss that Janice gave to my father. Now I'd like to thank her. But at the time I was only mortified. It may not seem much to you now, but at that time such scandal would zoom all up and down the whole area like a blue arsed fly. I was in a state of pure shock, running the wrong way down that road.

See up until then I had the idea that my Da was great. It's true he did shout and roar and get drunk, but I was his own big girl. It's also true that he would always try to cuddle and pet me, and me Ma would go mad and I would hide me face and blush. But when I thought of that now I felt somehow sick right down to my guts. So I stopped running and I walked, and I walked right round the block. I was afraid of arriving to school early and meeting the others.

I took it hard alright, my Da getting off with Janice. My head was racing and the whole of me youth took on a quite different light in a flash. I arrived at the school gates before I knew it and stopped. Afraid to go in and afraid to be late. I hated that school and I hated the gossiping girls. And for the first time I began to hate my Da.

One thing I did know about was hating, and me only a young one. I screamed and fought back since I was a baby. I was a bad girl, a menace, a messer and a mischief maker. My folks were just as bad, me Ma and Da got on together like a riot on the Falls. And I hated Sister Bernadette so much I had to bite my tongue sometimes, to stop me getting up and throttling her!

Well, my feet carried me through those big black gates alright, but it seemed like me life lay in ruins behind me. There was a big lump in my throat and I was muttering Hail Marys to stop myself crying. When I got to the class it had already started, but I knocked and walked straight in.

"Excuse me please" I said, and Sister Bernie glanced up at me, with her quick ratlike eyes. Tricia Connors was up reciting poetry. That nun saw I was in bits alright and she seized her chance.

"Next, Linda Green" she said.

Now one thing I was proud of was me memory, and I never forgot anything. That is if I bothered to look at it at all. But this day I stopped and stuttered, and me mind went blank with fright. It was stupid really, like everything in school, we learnt off all this poetry without understanding a word of it. Anyway, there was this awful silence. Then Sister Bernie prompted me, and I said a line but couldn't come up with the next. She'd used to come down with a ruler, and with the edge on your knuckles. It was a rare treat to catch me and down she came, whack, whack, and me stammering and starting to cry. Again, again from the start - and I had to start all over, it was only brutal.

Well, I was a lovely big girl for my age, as my Da used to say, and Sister Bernie was a short shrivelled hag of a woman, I made two of her. And me coughing and crying and stopping, and the others all silent with terror. Suddenly I felt sick but I didn't dare say it.

Then it happened. I can see it now, what a fucking horror. I gasped and I felt it coming and I couldn't stop it, and she ... whack ... underneath. And I coughed and whoosh ... like a bleeding yellow volcano. I puked on Sister Bernie, on her head and all down her habit, and a bit on Rosaleen and all over my books and my desk. I was only after eating my dinner.

Sister Bernie squawked and Rosaleen screamed and ran for the door, I was still sobbin and choking. Sister Bernie dragged me out of the class, the rest were dumb with horror, and gobs of meat and potato in her hair an down her neck. It was only long after that I could see anything funny in it. But I heard all the rest, excepting Rosaleen, thought it was brilliant, and they made a laugh and a mock of Sister Bernadette behind her back. They call her Sister Puke in the school to this day an it serves her right.

She marched me down the corridors to the sick room, I was shaking with shock and she with anger. I sat down in the chair as she began to clean herself off with a paper towel, giving out yards to me all the time.

"Get up off that chair" says she, but I wasn't listening.

"Get up you dirty little brat!" she went to give me a slap, but I turned my head and she hit me in the eye.

"Fuck off!" I screeched half blinded.

"Now we hear it" she said. "Now we hear the filth coming out", she was spreading vomit down her neck with the paper towel.

"You touch me again", I said "and I'll break your fucking neck".

"You'll suffer for this" she spluttered, "You and your thieving brother and your whoring father".

Then she went to belt me again, but I lifted me arm, and somehow I'd risen out of the chair before I knew it, and brushed the blow aside. She stepped back. Her face suddenly white. As I let fly a punch. Straight into her nose. I watched her totter and fall back on her bottom. Then I just stood there looking as she tried to get up, and half crawled, half ran out of the room, gibbering and clutching at her bleeding nose. It was a vicious belt I gave the nun that day.

As I say, I just watched her go, dead calm, like in a dream, and I watched myself walk to the basin and splash cold water on my face. Walking through the open door. Down the dark panelled corridor. Out the front door. Past the big board listing the Head Girls. Down the gravelled drive like a sleep-walker. I never turned my head and no one followed. Just as I was coming to the gate I heard this shout from behind me.

"Linda Green come back here!"
But I didn't turn a hair, just kept walking...crunch, crunch, crunch, down the drive. Then again.

"Come back here this minute!"
Suddenly I felt the eyes of half the school, staring down from the classrooms at my back as I went through the gates. I felt a rush of pure joy, thinking I'd done something great after all. Then I stooped and snatched up a bunch of the first daffodils, which grew there under the tree, and I turned round and waved the flowers at the old grey building. The white faces at the windows. The head nun a the door. Then a hop and a skip, and around the corner laughing.

I had a conviction right then that I'd left that school forever. If they didn't throw me out they'd have to drag me back roaring. I stuffed the flowers in the bus stop bin and walked quickly up the road. Just then I started to think again about my father. And I thought maybe I was a bit hasty, sure wasn't he always chatting up women, and maybe he was only giving her a lift and what harm. Janice could've kissed him just to start more nasty gossip. And I swore revenge. But I thought I might as well check up, crafty bitch that I am. so I went into Devenny's shop, and I looked up the Bottle Factory and Maxine's Hair Salon in their phone book. Then out to the phone box on the corner and I tapped out the first number... "No It's Miss Martin's afternoon off"... Then I rang the factory and sure enough....."Sorry Mr. Green takes a half day off on Tuesdays".

Well, that was proof enough for me. But funny enough I felt better then, pleased with meself and thinking how I could trip him up and all. And I pulled leaves off of the garden hedges as I walked and threw them into the wind.

When I think about me Da now I couldn't care two shits what he done. He was made redundant the year after and he slowly drank himself to death. But I was only young then, and even when I hated him I still loved him, if you know what I mean. Even if he battered me I believed in him. You'd swear by the way I went on that the sun shone out of his arsehole.

By the time I got home me good humour was gone. In I went by the side door, and me heading for me bed. But there was me Ma in the clean little kitchen feeding the baby. And there was Mrs. Geraghty from down the road drinking tea. If anyone thinks I got any sympathy from my ma they're much mistaken. Such a mean faced back biting hypocrite was never seen in that street before nor since. We fought like cats and prods, me an her. Though you'd have to pity her sometimes.

"What are you doin out of school?" she demanded as I came in the door.

"Nothing Ma, Sister Bernadette sent me home sick"

"Sick" she glanced triumphantly at Mrs. G, "Sick! You're no more sick than the devil himself! Where did you get that red face child and don't be telling me lies."

"I am sick" I protested, sitting down and starting to cry.

"Stop that snivelling girl" says she, and yanked me out of the chair, "Tell me the truth now before I beat it out of you."

Well I couldn't fool my Ma for long, and she shaking me like a rabbit. So I had to tell her, like, that I puked on Sister Bernie, and hit her back and all and ran out of the school. When she heard that she lost her head altogether, and flew off into her temper as I expected. Roaring and shouting and giving out miles. Such a litany of griefs! And old Mrs. G nodding all the while, nose in her tea. How all her children turned out bad and herself old with worry and us a livin disgrace, and God's house and her brother a curate an Danny caught robbin and her cross to bear, and now me destroying the good name and six children to rare, and she dare not show her face in the street for shame. And the baby screeching louder all the while.

Oh, she was ragin all right. She'd snort once in a while, like a heifer, and tap me across the ear, then off she would go again. When she got like this there was no stoppin her, so I just lay over the table and pretended to cry, staring about the sterile kitchen and getting madder and madder myself.

So what happens next. Oh fuck, it's years ago but I hardly dare tell it. Didn't she start going on about my Da, you know, him slavin away all his life to bring us up respectable, and the Sacred Heart of Jayzus, and he a real credit, having risen to assistant sales manager in the bottle factory. And the likes of me and Danny and Frances, lying and stealing and, Lord have Mercy, throwing up over a nun, and "Wait till your dad hears about this" and so on and some such crap.

If she knew what I'd seen that day she'd never have started goin on about my Da!

Now all this time Mrs. Geraghty was sitting up the end of the table supping her tay, and nodding and grunting the odd time. And me getting more and more desperate. Next thing her flabby jaws went tight, and her runny eyes went bright, and you could almost see her prick up her flesh old ears. And the baby screamed louder, if that were possible.

Cos at that moment I did get up off my chair, and me shaking and waggin my finger over Ma. I was bigger than her even then.

"Don't you tell me about my fucking Da" I shouted. "You know well he's not at work, and he's never at work on a Tuesday afternoon."

"Wh what" she said, taken aback.

"Your precious man" I sneered "went off whoreing this afternoon with Janice Martin. And if you don6t believe me you can ring up and check!"

"Wh what' - she said again, leaning on the table
And I knew suddenly that it was true, and I knew she knew, but didn't know what to say. She was stuck for words, my Ma, for the first time ever. And so was I, it was over, we could've gone to each other then and hugged and comforted each other.

"Oh Ma" I said, crying.

Then Mrs. Geraghty moved, and me ma's head jerked sideways like she'd been shot.

"Liar" she bellowed, "Liar" she shrieked "Get out of my kitchen before I kill you."
Then she lifted the baby's bottle from the table, and it crashed in smithereens on the black door closing behind me.

And still little Kathy roared.

What a day. I run straight up to me and Frances room, slammed the door behind me, threw myself down on the bed and cried and cried. I don't know what the old bitch said to Mrs. Geraghty, but I knew she was in a tight corner. What I said was the truth, but to say it in front of that mouth was something like high treason. I was sorry I said it too, and I just lay there a long time feeling brutal. I pulled the blankets round me, it was always freezing there, and thought of all that had   happened, and blubbered some more and half dozed off.

When I woke up I could hear me Da's voice and plates clattering, so I knew they were having tea. But I wouldn't go down. I cold hear the kids,

and my Ma and Da shouting and I strained to hear but I couldn't make out
the words. Then my heard jumped in my throat, and I cowered in the bed. I
could hear me Da, it had to be him, coming nearer, plod, plodding up the
stairs. I pulled the covers up so I could just peep out, hoping he was just
going to the jacks.

But then the door banged open, and in he walks, bold as brass and
smiling. So I knew that me ma hadn't told, like, that we knew about Janice.
The poor old thing was afraid of him 'n all.

"Hullo there me little flower" says he, and me pretending to sleep. He
staggered slightly, and sat down on the bed, panting. A big man with a puffy
red face. But where I used to think his jowls were manly, they now looked
disgusting, and where I used to think his thinning hair distinguished, it now
looked greasy and rotting.

"Are y'all right luv" he went on, his big sweaty hand on me face.

"I'm sick" I said, "leave me alone."

"Did you have a bad day at school" he cooed, hauling me up like a sack
and examining my red cheek in the half light. Blowing stale beery breath in
my face.

"I'll get that nun for this, I'll have the bleeding law on her."

"No Da please, I hit her too."

Then he took me in his arms and pulled me close and patted me. I swear
I was suffocating and crying a bit. And he crooning and rocking me, and
belching so his stomach lurched.

"You're all right, girl, you're all right" he was patting me back. And his
other elbow jiggling me tits, the big randy bastard. Maybe Janice wouldn't
have him. That was it! I saw through me father now all right, but he was a
big man, and I was as weak as a kitten in his power.

"You're all right luv, you're all right"

"Let me go" - I said, struggling feebly.

"You're all right" says he again with a squeeze. Then his big hand fell
between my legs. For a minute I done nothing, I was so shocked at his
fucking nerve, holding me and starting to stroke me there.

I suppose he thought that would excite me, and he was dead right. Cos I
started to struggle, but he held me, so I started to panic, and scream like I
was taking a fit.

"Shut up" - me Da hissed, shaking me, and his hand clamped over me
mouth. But I was past shutting up. I twisted, and bit hard into his hand, then
I screamed and I screamed again.

Then he hit me, an unmerciful wallop across the head. I didn't even see
it coming.

All I remember was falling down and down, and me head ringing like a fire engine, and faraway my Ma calling up the stairs and he was gone.

Well, I've been hit before, many's the time before and since, but when that pig hits you you can't forget it so quick. I crawled back over to the bed, and leaned against it, dizzy and shaking. And I wouldn't have got up at all only for the hate and shame and fury boiling over inside of me.

I got to my feet and staggered into the bathroom. Locked the door and sat down on the jacks, head spinning. Then I mopped my face but there was no blood, just a big red swelling and back eye coming. I looked like a boxer after ten rounds. After that I got out a fag from my secret hiding place, and Ilit it up then and there. Why should I care. I could hear me Ma washing the dishes and the television blaring downstairs.

Then I peeked out and tippy toed down stairs and out of the front door, closing it quietly behind me. It was still light, out I went through the front gate, where Scamp lay gnawing at a bone, and off down the road, my poor head throbbing like a train. It was great to get out of that house.

two **max, maggie & barney**

I didn't want to go back, so I just walked on and on down by the old canal. It was freezing cold, you'd think it was mid winter, and I was wishing vaguely that I'd brought my coat. But I didn't care really, till it started to rain. By the time I got to the bridge it was coming down hard, so I turned to the right out of the bitter East wind, and mingled with the people and the traffic. Everyone rushing and queueing. But I wasn't going any place, and it was no evening for strolling. I started to feel more and more discouraged, walking up that street, with all the flashing lights and machines roaring past me, and the rain turning to sleet. My hands and my head were going numb, I was cold and hurt and going nowhere. And after a while it started to really get to me, I saw myself, a funny two legged creature slogging through an artificial canyon, very real, very hard, and I saw, one foot after the next, just how far I would go, before I'd stumble and hit the cold concrete, the staring meaty faces closing around. Those faces, strange and savage, pushing past, staring past me, the lights, flashing and reflecting, hooting, the roar of heavy engines, and always sirens, near and far away.

Just then I came to a pool hall and walked in boldly. It was warm and dark and there were even kids in there. I hid in the jacks for a while, then pronounced myself fit, and found a stool by a heater in the corner. For a while I just watched the pool players, preparing their shots. Their faces would screw up with concentration, then click, clack, and plop in the hole. And then on to the next ball. I fumbled in me pocket for change, counted it, and bought ten fags, then back to my stool and lit one up, just ignoring everyone and hiding my damaged face behind my wet hair. Perched over the heater like a boiling fowl and then steam rising off me.

I wouldn't go home. I'd die first. But where could I go that they'd never guess? I thought of this guy Barney who used to run our summer play scheme, he used to help the kids out in trouble with the law and that. No good, I didn't know where he lived. Barney Maguire, but I knew where his sisters lived!

Next thing I was up and out the door, running through the wet snow to the phone boxes. And as I ran the yellow street lamps came flickering on, turning the sleet into swirling clouds of gold.

"Are you okay?" asked Barney, as the car almost stalled and pulled away.

"I thought you weren't coming."

"I had to get a push start" he glanced at me sideways" I'll run you back home if you like."

"No please Barney, I'm quite okay" - but I was feeling pretty dizzy, so I just put me head on me knees for a minute and stared into the starry darkness. The little old car putted in and out of some side streets, and before I could get me head straight we arrived at Barney's.

"Come on up and get warm then" says he, "you're in a woeful state". So I fumbled with the handle, and got out into a puddle. But when I saw the big grey block I hung back in the pelting rain.

"Come on" he took my hand. "You know me, I won't touch you I promise". I followed him up the big wide steps, looking about, flat footed and guilty, like a kid whose after falling in the canal. Then he had opened the huge door, into the high hall and up the empty stairs. Leaving wet footprints behind me, clutching my wet cigarettes and matches in me dirty red hand.

Then I thought - "This is the beginning of my new life!" I looked up, and there were strips of wallpaper and plaster hanging out of the ceiling. We came at last to a door marked 13 and went in, it was warm and bright inside. Posters and books and mess everywhere. A dirty orange carpet and a radio playing.

There I sat, in Barney's baggy clothes, over the little electric fire.

Supping sweet coffee with a drop of whiskey in it and feeling quite recovered. The flat was a dump, but it was least bright and cosy. Then Barney came back in and sat down in the armchair leaking stuffing (the chair not him!).

"So what are you going to do?" says he, and I looked back square into his dark eyes.

"I'm going to get a job and a flat of my own" I said.

Barney looked at me, quizzically, but said nothing.

"Listen I know you think I'm silly, cryin and everything. But I just had a bad day that's all". Still he said nothing. "I'm not going back home, not ever. If you'll just let me stay a few days I'll be alright". He raised his eyebrows still further.

"It's a small city, they'd probably track you down. How old are you anyway?"

"Eighteen" I lied.

"Come off it Lindy."

I was thinking - "Oh fuck it he's going to throw me out."

"Well I'm going to change my appearance" I said "I'll look quite different you wouldn't recognise me I swear". I was getting desperate.

"I'll even cook for you."

He laughed then, shaking his head.

"Listen, first thing we'd better contact your dear parents and .."

"I'm not going back" I squeaked. There's nothing left don't you see"

"I know I know" Barney raised his hands. "Sure didn't I run away from home meself, and I didn't get battered."

I put me hand to my cheek. It was all swollen up. I must have looked like a red balloon on a string. But I knew I was winning.

"That was Sister Bernie as well as me Da" I said "and I battered her'n all."

"You beat up a nun?" he laughed.

And I nodded and opened my blue eyes wide.

"Listen, what I meant to say was this, you can hide out here for a few days if you like, and no obligations, or I can fix you up to stay with friends. This isn't exactly the safest place in the world. But you'll have to get in touch with your folks, and at least give then a decent story, or they'll have half the country out looking for you."

"What can I say?" I said, but I had a good idea already.

I was lying on the carpet trying to look at a magazine. It seemed very late. I stretched out me body in front of the hot little fire and yawned, and wriggled inside the great woolly jumper, pleased with myself. My Da would go mad of course but what could he do. Especially now everyone knew he'd beaten me up. He had lost one of his prize possessions and it served him right. I yawned again. Over in the corner Barney was sill writing furiously. He was doing this paper on the potentialities of words, fuck knows why, claiming that our very words, our ordinary phrases, hold us fixed in a society where we are functions, objects and subordinate clauses. Next thing I must have dropped off, cos I vaguely remember Barney lifting me over to the bed, which was a mattress by the window, and turning off one of the lights. I lay there, half awake, a long time, me head throbbing and Barney still scribbling away. Staring up at the cracks in the ceiling and whole incredible day running over and over in my sleepy head. Barney's wrong, I thought, it's not words but pictures. Pictures flashing in me head.

An image of Janice's arm going round me Da's shoulders, and her big lips going out to kiss him, splash on the cheek. A picture of my Ma struck dumb for the first time ever, then a flash of Sister Bernadette, clutching at her bloody face. And me drunken Da again, drooling over my bed. Then one of myself, running out to the phone box, in the suddenly golden snow.

I was going to sit up and tell Barney and I was too lovely and warm and I must have blacked out then, I was fucking exhausted.

I knew there was something strange going on before I even opened my eyes. I blinked once, and saw these strange flowery curtains, the dawn light coming through and they fluttering. And there was someone strange in the bed behind me and it wasn't my brother Frances.

Then I remembered everything in a rush, my heart jumped and me head buzzed. I was free and alone in the world, scared and excited, I had to think fast and make plans. I had lashed out at everyone and run away, but I didn't care a shit and and I wouldn't go back, not ever. There I lay in bed with this Barney. But I was more thrilled than afraid, lying back and thinking, and blowing puffs of white warm air towards the high cracked ceiling. My whole life stretched out before me like a new empty house. For once in my life I was free, or anyway I felt free, which is all that counts. Like you feel for a few moments on rare occasions, like after quitting a job you hate, or walking out through prison gates. But other times I had fixed plans, commitments and stubborn purpose, and I've never really felt as free and elated as I did that morning. So full of hope unbroken and full of illusion. It's hard to describe what I mean. I was only young at the time.

First thing I needed was a haircut, and to dye my hair, brown or red? Then I'd have to find a way of getting my clothes and stuff, and then money... Barney would just have to help me, that was all. That big mound curled up beside me, like a giant hot water bottle with hair sticking out the top. It seemed exciting and dangerous being in the bed with him. Every now and then he'd snort in the pillow like a pig. Till I giggled out loud and he half woke up, groaning and turning over..I didn't dare move..and slipped his arm over me, snuggled up close, and sighed and went back to sleep. As I say I didn't dare move. Hadn't he promised he wouldn't touch me. Then I thought "maybe he thinks I'm someone else" and I almost giggled again. We were just leaning up against each other, between the smooth cool sheets, and it felt quite warm and nice, as I'm sure you might guess.

I lay there for a long time, my cheek on Barney's warm arm, like a big cat dreaming. and thinking all the while how I might get work and a place to stay. I could have layn there forever with Barney, feeling his breath in me hair, rising and falling like a calm summer sea. After a while moved quietly closer. Or did he? It's hard to tell, so our bodies just breathed together, and I could hear his heart, thump, thump, and my own thump, thump, thumpety thump.

Then the alarm clock went off, real loud. Barney groaned, and rolled out to stop it. Then he leaned back and kissed me on the cheek.

"I have to get up, there's someone calling for me at eight."

When I saw him, all hulky and naked, I giggled out loud, I couldn't help it. He must have been embarrassed too, cos he turned quickly and started struggling with his trousers. Then he tip toed through the dirty clothes and cups, and put on the kettle and the fire.

"You were talking in you sleep" he said.

"Oh? What did I say?" I sat up.

"Ah just moaning, like, and saying NO NO like as if you were fighting off a herd of crocodiles."

"That must have been my Da" I laughed.

"I'll probably be all day out" says he "There's spare keys here if you're staying around."

Just then someone banged on the door and walked straight in, it must have been open. I went to hide under the covers but it was too late.

"Hullo where did you spring from " says he, and a bright red head of hair on him.

"This is Peter, this is, um, a friend of mine. And you never saw her OK." Peter crossed his heart, rolled his eyes and winked at me.

"Pleased to meet you. Just call me Max" says I. The name just came to me then and I've been called that ever since.

Peter sat down and they chatted and poured tea, and I sat up in the bed, pulling the blankets around me. Peter offered me a fag and I took it. Barney tut tutted like an old hen, he hated cigarettes. Then the two of them rushed off without even finishing their tea.

"Make yourself at home" says Barney going out "There's keys on the table and food in the cupboard".

And they clattered off down the stairs.

For a minute I just stared at the closed door. Then I jumped up, my blanket around me, and locked the door and sat down in front of the fire and I thought "I am free and alone and safe in the anonymous city." It was a big high square room. The clock said half past eight, and I thought then of me folks and the kids at the breakfast table. Me Da would be going mad, he would go out looking for me. They'd of got the messages I rang and left with the neighbours, and the kids and Jamesy next door would be talking. And soon all the neighbours and girls and the nuns at school would be gossiping and speculating about me, the scandal of the day. I felt famous! Then I was up on my feet, and I put on a record and started to dance about, giggling and laughing like a drunk, swirling the blanket round and around. Till I collapsed in a dizzy heap on the carpet.

After that I put on Barney's baggy clothes and romped about, making porridge and boiled eggs and toast, I stuffed myself I was starving. Then I cleaned up the whole place and swept the carpet, I found a pair of scissors, took down the mirror and proceeded to cut off my hair.

That was a nasty experience, all right, for a vain young woman like myself, the scissors were blunted and I had to hack away for ages. When I was finished at last it was certainly different. I looked like a tinker after a fight. Then I took the keys and went out, feeling pretty strange and obvious. But in the streets everyone ignored me, which suited me just fine. It was only later I came to hate all the city people ignoring each other, they'd walk straight past if you were dying in the street. Everyone stuck in their little flats and houses and their dead end jobs, and all the petty and untold jealousy and loneliness, and landlords and bosses rakin in the cash.

So off I went in my new disguise, I managed to catch my brother Danny on his way home for the lunch break, and I bribed him to bring me a bag of my gear and my post office book which had some money in it. I spotted a gang of girls I knew from school, but I avoided them, and I sneaked down by the canal to wait, down on the wet bank amid the weeds and broken prams and rubbish.

I stayed down there, hidden, a good while passing time, and the city rushing on all about me. After a while I started thinking, about home and school and about my life, and I started coming up with some awkward questions. I felt like I was caught between the life I knew, and the unknown future alone, and at that moment I belonged nowhere, nowhere at all. Just a pair of eyes following ripples in water. What was I and why was I there? It seemed suddenly to me that everything was in fact pointless and hopeless, and everyone just passing time and hiding from the truth, that we're going to be dead and gone and soon forgotten. The ripples go on regardless, and the thrum, thrum of the cold traffic passing. I couldn't in fact give a meaning or see a real reason for going on. And still I sat there crouched by the stinking canal, crying a little, my salt tears dripping in the black mud and my mind drifting far away. The moment passed, I was young and strong, and shook away the tears of futility and despair. If I could see no meaning I could at least go out and seek for one, that's logic enough, I'd learn and watch everything to discover or invent something worth living for. I only really decided to leave home then, when I'd already gone.

The ripples become little waves, and the wind rushes the weeds. I was cold, but much stronger and I would not go home, unless I was caught. So I pulled myself together, and wiped my face and set off to meet Danny. I waited round the corner so as I could run, if me ma had got him and came down instead.

I spent a lot of time, those first weeks, up in Barney's bedsitter, mostly hanging around, listening to music and reading. Barney had loads of books and I started to read them all, But I soon found this was impossible seeing he didn't care tuppence for his own property, people would just take them away, and he always brought back more that he borrowed or robbed. Barney used to pick up people much like he picked up books, no offence to him, he liked to be in a gang to escape his depression and he would always be bringing back friends or freaks or old guys or anyone at all, to smoke dope and make music and drink and talk the night away.

But that first day when I came back with my bag it was empty an quiet. The bell did ring a few times but I was afraid to answer it. Barney never showed up and eventually I went to bed. But about two in the morning he crashed in with a whole crowd of people. I just pretended to be asleep, peeking out and watching them as they sprawled about and argued politics and shouted and laughed. When I woke up again they were all gone. Just scattered bottles and butt ends to prove it wasn't a dream.

How could so many noisy people leave, all together and so early? Where had they gone to? "Who knows, who cares" I thought, but I felt somehow a bit lonely, as I dressed and cleaned up their mess. I found an odd cigarette and lit it, and put on the music, but I still felt empty inside. Then I dragged up the big window and leaned out. It was a beautiful morning.

You could see quite a lot from that window, it was a high house, and looked back on a clutter of garages, gardens and lanes. After a minute a ray of sun peeped out from behind a chimney pot, and seconds later the windowsill was flooded with warm yellow light. It was a big wide window ledge, and mossy, and a nice place to sit in the mornings if you weren't afraid of heights. I was still leaning out, hearing the black-birds singing loudly over the traffic, when somebody rapped on the door.

"Hey Barney it's me Maggie" - came a mellow female voice.

I didn't move, but the record was still playing. The knock came again then I heard a key going in, and a woman walked into the room. I can see Maggie still, that first time, coming sudden in the door, and I wish she was still alive now. A big tall red haired woman, wide mouth, a few freckles, wearing a worn orange coat and bright yellow trousers. I looked at her speechless, seeing spots from looking at the sun.

"Oh sorry" she said, seeing me at once. "I was looking for Barney." I wanted to speak and talk and welcome her, but somehow I couldn't come out with a word.

"I'll go" she said, turning.

"No wait" I burst out. "There's tea made here in the pot won't you stay a minute."

The woman turned, opening her wide smile.

"Why not" she said, nodding. "My name's Maggie."

"I'm Max, er, and I know what you're thinking, that I'm chasing after Barney but its not true" - I had this idea that she was his girlfriend.

"Well I'm, not chasing after him either so we're quits. I'm just an old friend who lives down the road."

She took her tea, and cupped it in her hands, and took a sup and sighed.

"So what brings you to this part of the world?" says she.

But I kept my silence, looking in my tea, and trying to think up a good story. Then I looked up, and suddenly into, her warm orangey eyes.

"You can trust me, you're my sister" she said strangely, and stranger still I began immediately to tell the true story. It seems like Maggie was the first really honest person I'd ever met, and I took to her immediately, as if I'd always been waiting to meet her.

I started to tell Maggie the truth, as I saw it, and it wasn't easy. I ended up cryin on her shoulder, and getting me black eye bathed with a hot flannel, and laughing together and huggin each other and making more tea. With Maggie I became myself, hard and soft all at once. Maggie my friend who showed me my own way in the big cruel city. She was originally from the West, but lived in a rented house with six other women, one man, three kids and a dog. It was as if I had at last met normal people, she wanted to talk everything out clear and care for everyone, and to each according to her needs, they all seemed to have the same way of going on. We used to have great gas, me and Maggie, the way she'd tell a story would have you in knots laughing for hours. She was a waitress and she worked in a posh restaurant at nights. Well anyway, eventually the talk came round to Barney.

"The reason I came up here" she said "as to see is he all right."

"He seemed okay to me, though I hardly know him really."

"Yeah well, he got into a fight the other night down at our house, and he beat up two poor eegits who were plastered drunk."

"What, I never would have thought he'd hurt a fly, sure the kids used to walk all over him."

"Yes well" Maggie sighed, then leaned forward. " I'll try and explain him for you. See he was always the odd one out, well, he was in a couple of different things, like Nationalists, but he left, or he got thrown out cos he wouldn't take orders and the discipline."

"Is that what the fight was over then?"

Maggie was pouring more tea, shaking her head.

"Maybe yes, he was doing some stuff for..for this underground group, and now it seems like he's backing out scared, only really its cos he thinks they're not going any place, and they're Stalinist bastards any way. That's his problem, also I suppose bein on the dole in this kip and the Branch after him and..all more than that its hard to explain."

"Jeezus Christ"-.

"That's why I dropped over, to see is he all right."

"Can't he see all them gangs are no good" says I.

"I dunno about that, they're not all bad either, sure they've little to gain now, and everything to lose."

"Who do you follow then?.."

"Me?" Maggie chuckled. "I'm not in any Party, never will be, see I'm a feminist and I wouldn't work with them power freaks if you paid me, I think Barney's right about that..still, you end up helping them out" she paused, then stood up, gesturing, "Enough anyway" says she, "enough stupid politics, sure none of them have a clue about us, or work, or kids, or anything important."

"I never really thought about it" - I said - "The subject just never comes up."

"Of course not" says she "Listen I have to go."

But I wanted her to stay, to go on talking, about anything just so long as she stayed there.

"I have to go" she said again, and emptied her cup at a gulp "Tell you what, would you like to come over for tea."

"Thanks very much" I said. "Yes I will."

Its funny now to think back to that first day, when I first went down to Maggie's house for tea. I was pretty nervous all right, going down there by myself, with me schoolgirl clothes and me black eye. It was a lucky break for me all right, meeting up with Maggie. It was as if we became old friends in five minutes.

Their house was big and old and crumbling, set apart by itself among trees. An old woman had let it out to the "young ladies", she died soon after and they were thrown out. Its gone now. I found it by the number on the rusty gate and walked in, down the cracked pathway to a yellow painted porch. That house was something overlooked from another time, engulfed but not yet destroyed by the expanded city. I pressed the bell firmly but on one came. I was about to try knocking when a little tricycle came round the corner of the house pedalled with difficulty by a small child.

"Hello" - I said, and a pair of dark eyes flashed up at me. The child stopped.

"Who are you?" she said in a squeaky voice.

"My name is Max" I said "I've come for tea."

"Look at here" she held up a squashed worm in her tiny fist. "T'sa snake" she said.

"Yeuk" says I. "Sure its only a poor worm, why don't you let it go."

"No" she snatched back her hand. "It's mine."

"Tell you what" says I "I'll push you to the tree and we'll see does it climb up."

So off we trundled to the tree and hung the mashed up worm on a twig, but it never made a move.

"Let's leave it there and see does it wake up."

The tiny girl looked at me gravely.

"It's dead" she said, and her head jerked away "Push me, push me" she shouted, and "Vroom vroom faster" till we came right round to the back door.

"Derrie, tea time" a woman stuck her head out of the door "Oh hullo" says she.

Derrie jumped off the bike immediately and ran in past her.

"Hello", says I, "I'm Max, Maggie invited me for tea."

"Come in so, I'm Marie" she said, tossing back her long black hair, " you're just in time."

The back kitchen was long and low and painted bright blue. In the middle was big wooden table, and people milling around it. Drawing pots in clouds of steam, clattering knives forks and dishes.

"This is Max" Marie shouted. There was Maggie at the top of the table, dishing rice from a huge pot.

"You sit here by me" says she and kissed my cheek.

"Bring over the butter Marie."

"Where's the salt."

"Who's taken all the cups."

I took off me coat and sat. The other wall was covered over with pans on nails, posters, notices and hanging plants. In the middle was a smiling sun, red and yellow, saying "Nuclear Power, Fuck That" and others "Equal Pay for Equal Work" and "Legalise Abortion On Demand."

There was about a dozen of us. Janie and Tricia were telling this long story about a nasty manager, and everyone else was doling out food or diggin in. And so did I, I was hungry.

After that I used to eat there a lot, you could starve at Barney's place. They didn't seem to mind that I was always skint, I would put money in the Pot when I had it. I fell in with them anyway, and took my turn washing and cleaning and baby sitting. Everything seemed to me new and amazing that summer, I took to wearing their jeans and smocks and dungarees (not all at once), and Maggie got me a bit of work at the restaurant, before it closed down for good, and I went to their meetings and parties and demonstrations and met loads of people, and I grew up thinner and rounder and full of life and love.

But back to that first day, I was sitting down to eat, and Patrick, Marie's older kid, eyeing me across the table. The talk died, as we all tucked in, but this Patrick kept glancing, he had the same dark eyes as his little sister.

"Were you in a fight?" says he loudly.

"Don't be rude Patrick" says Marie at once.

But I felt myself blushing, staring at me plate, and there was this big silence, or so it seemed to me. Then I looked up, throwing back me hair that wasn't there.

"Me Da.."- I began, but Maggie had started to speak at the same time.

"Sorry go ahead" she said.

"Me old fella b'battered me" I was staring back at Patrick, "So I'm after leaving home."

I felt everyone looking at me, but I kept my eyes fixed on Patrick, he must have been about ten at the time.

"Ma Da's gone to America" he said, and turned back to his food.

Then I did the same, stabbing a carrot, as other conversations began and I grinned and looked about, I felt accepted anyway.

That's all I really wanted, then, to feel like I belonged. And never more so than that first day at Maggie's, with me black eye and my working accent, and blushing as red as the carrot on my plate. You forgot all that when you're old and hard.

After a while some of them rushed out, but more people arrived, and we all got poured mugs of home made wine and got a bit merry, laughin and joking. Some of them started playing cards, and Maggie took me up to her room. She let me rummage through her clothes, so I had a great time tryin everything on, throwing shapes and messing about. I ended up with a pair of bright green trousers and a pink woolly, my taste being pretty woeful at the time. I remember that room quite well, she had it done up like herself, all oranges and browns, and the big tree rustling outside. She found some music on the radio, and we drank our wine and talked. Maggie asked me loads of questions all right, but she never once told me I should go home. Then she had a go at me hair, trying to straighten out the spiky bits, and hugged me and said I was fine. She was very warm like that, was Maggie, but it never stuck me then of course that she was gay, which she wasn't really, cos she used to go with fellas.

But she really preferred women, as she said. Maggie had no hangups, about sex and that and talking about it, and I used to be secretly shocked cos I had plenty. True I hated the hypocrisy of the nuns and me Ma, and I was now turned off by the brute image of me Da, but still and all I'd taken in all kinds of notions of purity and guilt and submission and other shit, can you ever escape it?

"I'd better be off to bed" says Maggie at last, "I've to be up at the crack of dawn."

"I'll be off then," my heart sank at the thought.

"You can stay over if you want to" but I shook my head.

"Sure all me stuff's at Barneys ... I better go back."

"OK then, listen come over any time you can just walk in the back door." So I got my coat and she took me to the front door and hugged me and kissed me good night.

That night, walking back from Maggie's, I felt like I'd glimpsed into another world. As if Maggie had lifted up the corner of an invisible screen, peeping round and laughing at my surprise. I felt I was able now, to think and act on my own. I giggled out loud and my whole body thrilled, my feet bouncing off the cracked pavement. I felt like I was transformed, and my past life and deeds were just past history. I had escaped as well as run away.

The flat was in dark, but for a candle stub flickering. A dark figure crouched behind it.

"Barney?'" I shouted. "What's wrong?"

A head came up behind the table, it was him.

"What's wrong with the light?" I said

"Money" Barney grunted - "No cash"

So I fished in me pockets for change and put it in the meter. The light came on and then the fire. Barney was at the table writing on a big note pad. I put down me bag of clothes and took off me coat.

"How's life" I asked, off hand, but he ignored me. Then I was angry. I stood over him, hands on hips, but he didn't look up or stop writing. Then I saw that his words were scrawled, all up and down the page. His hand was going down again, to plunge into a new sentence. My hand went out, in a twinkling, and took the chewed biro from between his fingers.

For a moment Barney actually went to go on writing. Then he opened his hand slowly and stared at it, his head lifted and flopped back. Glazed eyes peered up at me from a million miles away. He coughed and gestured vaguely, tried to speak. He was spaced out, twisted, out of his tiny mind!

I dropped the biro and took a quick step back. He was laughing and staring and staring at my face, with a great sloppy grin of an idiot.

"You're beautiful" he said, reaching out.

"You stay away from me" I shouted, and he flinched back slowly.

"It's, it's OK I'm just having a little trip...here, here would you like a tab?"

"You must be out of your fucking head."

He was giggling, "I'm floating out of my head."

Well the whole thing seemed stupid and dangerous to me, and I was scared and angry. But after a while I could see that he wasn't violent, in fact he wouldn't say boo to a goose. Mainly he was talking rubbish, looking about at nothing in wonder or horror, he was going through this colossal drama, without ever leaving his chair. So I sat there at the table and took a sup of whiskey and listened to his ridiculous imaginings. It went on and on, Barney showed no sign of letting up. So I put on one of his records, which sent him into ecstasies altogether, so it went on and on, I got into laughing with him, or at him. Then he started rolling a joint, but he wasn't able for it. I finished it off for him but the bleedin thing came out bent, seein as I'd never rolled one before. That struck him as incredibly hilarious, and we laughed, and took puffs of it, and coughed and laughed some more. It wasn't that funny really. But it went on for hours.

Now every now and then Barney would shake his head clear for a second, and when he did that he looked to me smaller, older, and a bit worn down, hunched there at the table. He was sobering up a bit, but he looked terrible.

"What are you so depressed about?" I said, and his eyes went sharp.

"Who told you I was depressed?" he demanded

"Well you are aren't you?"

"Who told you that?"

"No one.. well, I was talking to your friend Maggie, I went there for tea."

"That bitch, she's always spreading gossip about me."

"No you're wrong" I said. "Anyway I like her."

We sat quiet for a while. Barney looked sick, rubbing his temples with his thumbs. It was getting very late.

"Do you want coffee?" I asked

"Yeah, listen Lindy I'm sorry, Maggie is OK, but a bit nosy sometimes."

Then I turned on the kettle, and the second bar of the fire, and put more money in the meter. Outside it seemed a bit less dark, but I was beyond feeling sleepy.

"So what has you so depressed?" I asked again, Barney sighed and scratched his head.

"I'm just a bit of a dead end, that's all" he said.

"How so?"

"It's just that things are so hopeless, I seem to be doomed to work and fight for hopeless causes. See I don't fit in, like, things I'd like to do I can't, cos of the way things are, now with the depression its even worse, if you know what I mean...I end up running in tighter and tighter circles. And all the time the Branch nosing about, like bleeding vultures just waiting for me to crack up.."

"What, are the police after you?"

Barney shook his head slowly.

"Out to get me" he said. "But that's normal, they watch everyone with any cop-on at all, no, my problem is, that with the way I took and the beliefs I hold, I got no way of going on."

"How do you mean?" says I.

"Ah it's not important. I don't want to be depressing you now, and you only starting out."

"No, go on" says I, he wanted to clam up.

"Remember that summer project where you met me" he said suddenly.

"Yes of course, I though it was good."

"It only lasted two weeks, Lindy, it was supposed to be all summer."

"Well it was better than nothing, the kids loved it."

"Oh sure" he said "what we wanted to do was OK, but as far it went, just to give you'se a chance to enjoy yourselves, and choose and decide a few things for yourselves."

"Quite right" I said.

"Right" says he. "Then didn't Father Damien jump in and ban the discos. And remember the so called discussion groups?"

"There only was one."

"Right, the parents stopped it because someone mentioned sex. And then the sports, the bleeding politicians poking their noses to claim any credit going. And when we told them to fuck off they stopped the grant, well it wasn't that simple but that's what it came down to."

"Is that why you're upset?"

"No no no" he was exasperated, "that was a small thing, what I'm saying is this, all those people and organisations are fighting each other for power, over some aspect of people which is their special corner, and they fucking force and brainwash people into obeying or knuckling under."

"You're right of course" says I, getting up cos the kettle was boiling.

"Remember Christy and Gollo" he said, turning in his chair.

"Bleeding hooligans."

"I suppose they were that, and young Katie with them, but they were only kids in that place who had a clue what had happened to them."

"I never had much to do with them, to tell you the truth."

"You weren't the only one, they weren't even let in the so called Youth Club."

"I forget, I never seen them after."

"They're in prison Lindy, lockup, Nick, and Katie, her Da nearly beat her to death, she's inside now and all, and Pado when he..."

Barney stopped abruptly, red in the face, as I handed him his coffee. Then he went on, once he got going there was no stopping him.

"I can tell you this much" he said "it's twelve year now since I left home and I was your age then, this whole country, this whole society is rotten through and through. There's just this thick fucking icing of respectability and religion and privilege..underneath that it's power games, anything you can get away with is right. You name it, they'll use moral blackmail, they'll use brute force, they can strangle you in bureaucracy or just blacklist you or stick you in an institution. And if all that fails they will beat you up, torture you, put you away, and all the while they're selling the place out and turning public misery into private cash." He paused, then plunged on. "See I know very well what's going on, and all these so called Revolutionaries are doin is building up more power mad organisations, in the exact same fucking mould, if you know what I mean. That's the way it always was, I suppose, only now the whole thing's falling apart, it can't go on much longer."

He stopped then. I was beginning to figure him out.

"Listen if its true what you say, then all you have to do is set up a new kind of organisation."

Barney tried to laugh, leaned back in his chair.

"That's logical enough" he said. "That's why they're afraid of people like me, cos I don't fit in their cosy little rat race, only they're wrong, I'm really confused and powerless."

"Well you shouldn't be" says I. "We're only waiting for something new, cos you're right, there's no work and nowhere to go, exceptin drugs and crime, and there's nothing even half decent, like, in the political line."

That was my first political speech. Barney grinned at me. But it was a forced grin, and as the silence lengthened, I could see he had a touch of the horrors. We didn't speak, but then I saw him for the first time as an old man, white face lined black under the naked bulb, his body all crooked, like a wounded bird shivering and twitching. His voice when it came, was a whisper.

"It's just gone too far with me" he said "and I've seen too much, like Flynner who got blown to pieces and Padraig who got shot twelve times and..or people destroyed quietly, so many people I knew. Some of them did find work, and got mortgaged and married, fair play to them and suddenly found they'd changed sides. You can talk all night, but its people you don't forget so quick. Like people who ended up in prison, Jayzes, when I start to think of them. And then Stevie, dead by his own hand...I can see now he was dead fucking right."

He stopped, grinning horribly, I thought he would cry soon.

"It's no good" he whispered "I'm stuck see, each day more I add a little bit to my fury and bitterness and fucking guilt. I can't take it anymore, just, just tricks and play acting and, and creative fucking self destruction. That's my trip Lindy, prison or the mad house or death for sure..I'm not a violent man, but when I try to sleep alone at night I notice I'm grinding my teeth, and then I hear this sound coming closer, the noise of machine gun fire, and I realise again its meself, firing blindly at everyone, the hot metal leaping and burning in me hands."

Barney stopped speaking finally. As sudden as he began. As if he had said everything he wanted to say. I just sat there. A blackbird had started singing out the back. Soon I was feeling heavy and sleepy again. Barney got up at last and kissed me on the cheek...

"Thanks for makin me talk" he said. "Don't mind me goin on like that."

"I want to know everything" I said, "but right now I need sleep."

Then the door bell rang. Loud and long.

Barney was off like a shot. Out the door. Down to the hall window facing the street. He was back.

"Special Branch" he said "looking for me."

The bell was ringing again. Barney was emptying ash trays. Stuffing papers in a rubbish bag.

"Listen tell them you're a battered wife, they know I work for them a bit."

"What? What do they want?"

"Nothing, search and question, take me in for a few days."

"I'll tell them you're away."

"They'd come in anyway."

He was still rushing about. The bell was ringing. And faraway a hammering noise began.

"Can't you hide then", I yelled. He stopped still.

"Well I have a place..if you think you can pull it off."

"I'll try it."

"Say I'm in England, delay them if you can" he was stuffing a suitcase now.

So I ran down the stairs. Frightened but excited. People were wakening up. Opening their doors.

"OK, I'm coming" I shouted, and a man banged his door cursing.

"Open up now."

"Who's there?"

"Police."

I put the high door on the chain and opened it slightly. Instantly a black toe was in the gap.

"What do you want?" says I.

"We have a warrant to search the flat of Mr. Bernard Maguire. Open up that door."

"He's left" I said "that's my flat now."

"Open up now, there's the warrant."

"Let's see it" my voice squeaked.

I examined it, slow as I dared, and it back out the gap.

"Listen I'm after leaving me husband an I just moved in here. I'm afraid you're his pals come to get me."

So one of them showed me an ID card, which took more time. They were getting furious.

"Open up now missus or we'll break that chain."

"I'm sorry it's my flat now not Mr. Maguire's."

There was a great crash as a heavy body hit the door.

"OK OK I'll open it" I shouted, and took off the chain.

The door swung back. I was bundled aside as four big men pounded up the stair well. Stupidly I followed them.

When I got there the room was dark. They were rummaging about, flashing torches. One torch flashed in my face.

"What's wrong with the fucking light?"

"Not working" I said. Barney must have knobbled it.

"I'll take a look upstairs" said one.

Then the bastards turned on me. Out of the blue. Grabbed me, crashed me up against the wall, torch in my eyes, I was terrified.

"Where's the cunt. Where's your lover hiding?"

"He's gone, gone to England."

"Where? What address?"

"What is your name?"

One pinned me to the wall. Another shone the torch. The third started digging at me, pinching me, pulling at me clothes.

"I don't know the address. Honest Ow. Stop it."

"You're a whore, you're a filthy bleeding whore."

"He's said he'd send it."

Then I was being shaken violently, head banging off the wall.

"You're a whore, say it, you're a whore, say it you bitch."

"I'm a whore" I croaked, holding in a scream. Hands were ripping down me jeans. Pawing at me.

"You suck his prick, say it you filthy whore."

"Hey Johnny take it easy" the first one had come downstairs, " there's just a student up there. Did you get her details?"

"This cunt won't talk".

"I will, I will" I squeaked.

"What's your name then?"

What's my name I thought.

"Janice" I came out with "Mrs Janice Martin."

"Right" said the first man, I saw a black gun in his hand,   "Your friend is a dangerous fucking subversive. Tell him we'll be back."

"He's gone away" I still protested, but he was busy flashing his torch and pointing that gun about.

"Come on lads, leave her, she's not worth it."

He backed towards the door. One of them spat in my face. The hands left me body at last and I slipped down to the floor. As I heard the boots stomping off down the stairs I burst into tears.

Next thing I was up, pulling me pants, and out to the window. I saw all four of them get into the car and leave. I leant on the cold glass shaking.

"Bastards, bastards bastards" I muttered over and over.
I watched the last police car start up and disappear. A thin grey dawn was creeping across the city.

Back inside to the fire. I was shivering and shocked. Soon after Barney came in the door, with his rucksack and bags and cobwebs in his hair. I was at the sink. Thought I would puke, tried to stop crying and began laughing wildly instead.

"W' welcome back" I blurted.
Barney unloaded and put back the light bulb.
"Did they hurt you?" he asked.
"Pigs" I said "Fucking bastarding pigs" and I changed back to crying again. Barney came over and put his arms around me.
"You're all right, luv" he said "You'll be all right."
I caught me breath. Then I was breaking away from him in panic. It was the exact same thing my Da had said to me.
"You're the same" I shouted "I'm not alright. They wanted to rape me!"
Then I lifted a cup and it flew, smashing against the mirror. And after that I set about wrecking the gaff.
It didn't last. There wasn't much worth wrecking. I broke two records and cups I think and the only good chair. Then I was back to the sink, throwing up.
When I finished with that and washed my face I felt better, and I looked around for Barney. He was squatting in a corner, head in hands.
"Listen" says he "Will I take you down to Maggie?"
I nearly forgave him when he said that, he wasn't the same really. I was quite OK, yet in another way, I'd never be the same again. I had puked their shit out of my system, but I still sat down, shivering on the floor.
"Can you make a cup of tea" I said.
"Yeah, listen I'm really sorry, I should've known what might happen, you should've been the one hiding."
"Have you got a fag" I asked calmer now, and he looked for one. "It wasn't your fault, them coppers are insane."
He handed me a half cigarette, then went for the kettle.
"Did you tell your name?"
"Course not. What, did you think I'd talk?" I was angry again.
"They could rape me a million times and I wouldn't talk. I said I'd left me husband. Made up a name."
Barney sighed. Slapped his own face.
"I'm sorry" he said "I was out of it, that was a stupid idea, they love that.."

"What, raping women?"

"Well, no, yes I mean, they couldn't have, if that's any consolation."

"They nearly fucking did."

"They'd love to I'm sure, only for O'Brien would have to stop them. See terror works both ways."

"What's that supposed to mean?"

"He knows if they raped you I'd go mad and blow his fucking head off,..and I would've tried, we'd probably both be dead.."

"What, do you have a gun?"

"I need one, at this stage."

Barney sat the two cups on the carpet, then lifted from a paper bag a black revolver. He dropped it back in.

"I was only waiting for you to scream" says he.

"What" I said "I almost did scream!"

I remember the sun streaming through the curtains. I got meself in the sleeping bag and zipped it up around me neck, ignoring Barney. After that night I learned easily to hate all police. They came the next week again but we were out. We left the flat soon after and went to live in a squat. Barney never did go berserk as he threatened. I wouldn't let him for one thing, and anyway we were too busy. We tried to change the whole world, me and him, but that's another story. I only wish we had succeeded and he were alive still.

three **macker mcdonagh**

Jimmy Quinn was aware of the crash of explosions. The faraway thunder of artillery. Then the rattle of machine guns, coming closer and closer. He lay curled like a baby, head buried in the mud. His breath came in short painful gasps. Something was stabbing him in the side. He began desperately trying to get up, but a black enveloping weight held him fast.

"Coward," his father cried. "Yer a yellowbelly coward."
Jimmy pulled together his last remaining strength, and heaved, but he couldn't move. A surge of panic swept over him, then faded slowly, with his Da's mocking laughter, the guns, the soldiers and the screams.

He opened his eyes then, and brought them into focus. He could see that he was lying in a room, amid heaps of plaster, bricks, bottles and scattered sleeping bodies. Jimmy moved his head, grimacing as a bank of pain leapt across his forehead. Blurred memories intruded, jemmying open a dark door, running together with crates of scotch and vodka. Then drinking, drinking for days and selling drink. Drunken fights and hoarse singing. He remembered moving on, always moving, from derelict sites to deserted streets to broken down houses.

Jimmy closed his eyes, groaned, and opened them again. He could make out the bodies of Bernard, Pato and Steamer, sprawled side by side in the center of the room. He supposed that was Janie and Carmody, tangled under the blanket by the wall. And he saw Macker McDonagh, propped by the broken window, head slumped, hugging his battered jacket to his skinny chest. Jimmy heard a steady drip, drip, and he felt the floorboards tremble with the roar of heavy traffic down the quays. But his eyes remained on Macker where he sat, and his cracked lips broke into something like a smile. Macker was thin, his clothes filthy, and his runners worn right through. But to Jimmy Quinn the sleeping figure was still alive and powerful. Liable at any moment to leap into life, joking, cursing and singing.

As Jimmy's eyes closed again, still smiling, his mind went back three days. He Pato and Steamer sat huddled by a concrete doorway in Maeve Street flats. It was just getting dark and he had been peering out across the misty, rain filled courtyard ...Heavy drizzle mingled with blue smoke, swirling down from broken chimneypots. The last street light, flickering, the broken swings and prams and the wrecked car, the great grey blocks of flats.

"C'mon Jimmy." Pato had said. "Are you playing or not?"

Then Macker had appeared, head down and running through the rain. Macker the clown, the chancer. Macker the hooligan. He had seen them and shouted out, then suddenly cartwheeled on the glass strewn tarmac, and bounced up the steps into the doorway.

"Howaya doin there lads, ah Steamer me old pal, is this the famous Maeve Street cardgame I see before me?"

"Two pair" said Steamer, not looking up.

"I'm out" said Bernard.

"Three sevens."

"Fuck all here." Jimmy had thrown his cards on the pile.

In a moment Macker had swept them up, constantly talking, as they flashed and flew across the concrete. It was magic, trick after magic trick.

"I'll tell you what, young fellas," Macker had said, "Would you'se fancy doing a stroke with me tonight?"

"A job? What's in it for us?" Steamer leaned forward on the step.

Macker had spread out his skinny arms. Shrugged his shoulders. As if, Jimmy thought, he would start juggling.

"What is it you fucking want?" he said, "I can promise you good crack, and even splits. A few bob and booze, loads of booze in fact. What more would you be wanting from life, tell me that?"

They had stayed silent, for long moments, as a gang of shouting children charged down the balcony above their heads. They didn't know Macker, but they knew his reputation. A showman, certainly, but a smart operator on top of that. Steamer's eyes glanced. Bernard nodded. Jimmy still remembered the tingle of excitement, action at last! He had nodded too.

Jimmy grinned, thinking back, then grunted with pain, as he rolled himself over, and lifted himself slowly from the bottle and brickstrewn floor. It had been a good robbery. A good few days away. Away from the family bickering in the little flat. Away from the brutal boredom of school. He realised that for months on end he had hidden himself in a sullen and silent rage. Now, despite his hangover, he felt power and life coming back. He felt for a cigarette and lit one, then he stood up and picked his way through the sleeping bodies and rubble to the broken window. Outside the rain had stopped, and a thin pale sun was piercing the murk. The yellow and green waters of the river slid past beneath him, on both sides the traffic was packed tight. Across the river he could see more deserted buildings and factories stretching away. The city centre was busy, and if you had work you could still do well, but all the time the army of unemployed and unemployable grew. That's what bothered him, he thought, the shiny offices, the rich gliding by in their big cars. No one even pretended any more that there was any future for his type. Jimmy pushed back his greasy hair and breathed in the cool polluted air. The Tech he was supposed to attend was a joke, everyone knew it. And there was no work, not on the building, not in the Council, nowhere, except maybe in the Coop, that was an idea ...

Looking down Jimmy saw an open backed van pull in out of the traffic and park on the pavement. He took no notice, as he watched the gulls, skimming the green waters for scraps of sewage. Two men had got out of the van, carrying hammers and crowbars, and began to prise the heavy boards off the front door. The first board moved with a loud crack.

Jimmy panicked, rushing around the room, shouting, shaking people awake.

"Get up lads, get up, there's fellas coming in..."

A few minutes later, and they were all out the back, picking their way, like crabs, across the muddy waste ground. All sleepy, ragged and staggering after three days drinking. they went on up the hill and between the tinkers' caravans, past the yapping dogs and the half starved children playing in the rubbish. Macker knew these people, every one of them was some kind of a cousin. He led the way through, aiming a kick at an aggressive pup, shouting greeting at a woman emptying a pot. But the woman ignored Macker McDonagh and he did not stop. He was a half traveller - 'Macker the Knacker' was the taunt. But he knew he had no welcome here, nor his father neither.

Out onto the street. On up to the gate of the Mansions. And Macker

stopped there, finally awake and feeling terrible. One thought occupied him
.. he must get away now to rest and think.

"Well now lads, it looks like the party's over" he said, looking on at the
crowd of children, skipping and darting about inside the gates.

"Hey lookat there's Macker."

"Hey Macker cumear."

In a moment the little gang were surrounded, but it was Macker whose arms
and jacket were seized.   Others, seeing the crowd, came running. Small
hands tried to prise the almost empty whiskey bottle from his pocket.

"The school is on strike Macker."

"Gis a sup of that."

"Ah go on Macker."

"Hey Macker come an do a show."

"Ah Macker do Elvis, c'mon Macker."

"Get off! Get off me!" he shouted, head down, "I'm not doin nothing
today, I'm in rag order!"

"Ah go on Macker." It was a small freckled girl, hanging out of his arm.
Macker saw her. Then looked up. The crowd had grown suddenly, the
children were milling about, calling his name. People were stopping to look
through the bent railings. Macker flicked back his mop of dirty hair, breathed
in deeply and grinned.

In a moment he was free of the grabbing hands, ducking out of the crowd
and running down wide steps into the courtyard of the big old flats. Where a
few tiny children were playing and a few women, tired and heavy, sitting out
taking the rare sun.

The kids had pursued him in a mass. Young fellas and girls shrieking.
Macker leapt up on the roof of a burnt out Cortina, a relic of the night before.
He stood there stock still. Legs splayed, bottle in hand. Then he roared in a
deep American drawl.

"Okay you Ladies and Gentlemen down there. Will you please take your
seats now in the places provided ... Now you young gents have got to stay
offa this here stage, or my bouncers here will eeject you from the theeaatre!"
Macker dropped his head, wiggled his hips, threw out an arm and was off!
Shaking and a hopping.

"Ain't nothin but a hound dog

Howlin all the while ..."

And the kids were laughing and squealing. The women walking over with
broad smiles. People were opening their windows and leaning over
balconies.

An air of Festival infested the grey flats.

Girls held hands and danced. Toddlers were lifted onto shoulders.

A flock of pigeons dived towards the green river.
Clean washing flapped in the sun.
> "Oh I'll do any thing
> That you want me to
> But hey ho honey lay offa my shoes..."

Macker was making an amazing noise. Crooning into his bottle.
Flapping on the fronts of his worn out runners.
> "Get off Get OFF
> Get offa my blue suede shooz..."

So it went on. Jimmy sat on the blackened bonnet clapping his hands.
Steamer and Pato were lifting down little kids, as they climbed up onto the
roof. Most had seen the show before. Macker could do Elvis, disco of
course, and plenty more impressions. Paisley, the Pope, he could do the
Queen till you cracked up laughing, and lots of acrobatic magic tricks.

"I am here to astound. I am here to amaze!" he would shout. And
because he was so small he seemed always to be mocking himself. He could
get away with anything like that, could Macker.

But this day he was exhausted. He could feel his head thumping and his
aching joints protest. Instead of the usual kick he got from the laughing
faces he felt a huge weary sadness creeping up on him.

"What am I doin here?" he was thinking, launching gamely into another
number. He had sworn to lay low for a while. The cops were onto him and
they had nearly caught him twice.

Then as if to confirm his fears, Macker saw three policemen coming
across the yard behind the crowd. A foot patrol, new to these flats and
always in threes.

Macker nodded to Steamer, feeling dizzy now, and suddenly angry and
desperate ... He stopped singing abruptly. Held up his hands for silence.

"Well now folks ah do think there's uh some thin funny goin on aroun
heeah. Ah do believe there's uh somethin rotten in this heeah
auditorium..Tell me, is there uh goddarn horse in the house?"
There was puzzled laughter.

"Naw, naw" Macker roared. "That aint no horse ah smell..What ah smell
is them thaar PIGS."

His arm flashed out, pointing. The kids turned, and drew back away from
them. The police looked embarrassed.

"That sure is a shameful thing to see" he shouted. "Them thaar Pigs
comin in here. Why only last night they bashed in poor Davey Driscoll's
head, way down in Fatima Mansions."

Macker glanced down to Steamer, Jimmy and the rest, his face white and
strained.

"Do I hear Pigs Out, come on now everybody..Pigs Out", clap, clap, clap, "Pigs Out" clap, clap, clap.

The children took up the chant. The older cop was talking to his radio. The others, young country recruits, tried to ignore it, one went beetroot red.

But the kids were edging forward, laughing and jeering, and as the cops backed off they closed in faster.

Next things the cops were running for the gate. Abandoning all dignity. A few half bricks and a Fanta bottle flying after them.

A low ragged cheering broke out, and echoed around the flats.

Macker was kneeling on the roof the the burnt out car, trying to shake his head clear. Now he must move fast. He would go the to the North side, away from here.

At that moment a plump, middle aged woman marched out from one of the stair wells, chair leg in hand, and followed by a reluctant man. It was Jacqueline McCann, red faced and furious, making straight for the car where Macker had performed.

"Hey Macker watch out." It was Jimmy.

"Get out!" she yelled, approaching, "Get out of these flats, Macker McDonagh. You're a living disgrace. You filthy bleeding criminal..Out, now! There's respectable people living here.."

Macker had jumped to his feet, still on the car roof, and watching that chair leg. The kids were running back. A new drama!

"Get out you little rat. I seen what you done. Them coppers come in here only doin their job. Get Out. Or God help me I'll beat you out. Lookat that car, someone worked hard for that car. Get out you bastard, corruptin our kids."

She was banging the chairleg on the roof. Macker had ducked his head, as if to let the torrent roll over him, but it went on and on, as the crowd gathered in, fascinated. Jackie paused at last for breath.

"Come on you'se." The man indicated Macker and his friends. "You know you're barred out of here."

"Em ah speaking" Macker took on a high English accent, "To a member of McGuigan mansions Tenants Association?"

"Shut up you filthy pig you, or God forgive me I'll kill you, you dirty little knacker comin in here. I pity the poor woman after rearing the likes of you, you.."

Macker's control broke. He was crouching. Screaming back at her. Spit flying. Arms waving.

"She's dead..dead dead you fucking old trout..you can keep your fucking coppers and your fucking stick an your stupid man, and you can stick them up your big fat arse hole!"

Jacqueline McCann threw the chair leg. But Macker was gone. And it hit young Damien O'Connell full in the face, starting another row which is going on to this day.

But Macker was gone, up the steps and out the gate. Gone straight down the hill towards the city. The children and the gang saw him go. Jimmy shouted and waved. Only this time nobody followed him.

Macker knew immediately that he was in no condition for running. Soon he slowed to a jog, stopped a minute, felt worse and continued at a slow walk. He was going down a street of squatted buildings, coming close already to the city centre. First office blocks, all glass and big 'TO LET' signs, with guards and dogs inside, then shops, banks and insurance companies.

Macker crossed an intersection, as the crowd grew thicker, and evil smelling vehicles filled the street, hooting and roaring their engines. The pavement was packed as well. Secretaries and pale office people, scurrying for their lunch, businessmen and shoppers. Large people, well fed and confident in their smart clothes. Macker felt sick. His stomach heaved and his eyes streamed, his small grey-blue figure weaved in and out of the crowd.

"Might as well be invisible, they'd walk right over you" he thought. And his mind ran back and ran back to the nasty scene at the Mansions. He felt quite alone and suddenly afraid. Looking about for police, and his tired body falling into a heavy depression. It seemed to be getting dark. He would go to the North side, disappear into the CoOp area, where he knew of an empty flat, a loose side window, a quiet back room.

Macker walked on, dizzy and sick, walked mechanically into the heart of the city. Past the big stores and fancy restaurants, past the line of beggars and junkies and over the river. He felt cold sweat now on his neck and forehead.

"What's wrong with me?" he wondered, panicky, as he joined a herd of pedestrians, surging at the lights. For a moment he was part of them, jostled, then stumbling free, past the hotels and the cinemas to the Fun Palace, where the machines flashed and rang, beckoning him in. Then bus queues, long lines of buses, more shops..He was thinking now of his Da, wandering these same streets after days and nights drinking, and back, years before, to him and his Da wandering country roads in summer. It was he who had taught him the trumpet, and the songs and the magic tricks. A violent man,he had always been gentle with Macker, only Macker could calm him in his drunken rage. And he would give Macker what he could. But now he was installed in the alcoholic unit of the mental prison.

Macker stopped, casually, and turned across the wide street, threading his way through the stalled traffic. He had spotted three cops on the next corner. Now he turned into a side street, still going north, and his thoughts turning, as they always did, to his brother and sisters, Damien, Kathy and Tricia. And he walked even slower, as another wave of sickness and despair swept over him. It had been left to him to take care of them, in that high squatted flat. Damien would be twelve now, Kathy about nine and Tricia, she might be six. His Da had wrecked that flat, twice, then came less and less often. But they had been all right, Macker knew it, for he was already a dab hand at robbing, and he knew how to unload. And anyway his Da would sometimes give them cash. It had been alright, Macker could look after them, only for the neighbours and the police, and Tricia letting on to that Social Worker. A strange child, Tricia, strange like his Da. Macker pictured her face, wishing now above all that he had never struck her. He kicked viciously at a Coke can, which flew out under a lorry and was squashed flat. They had come eventually, with the police, and had to break the door down to get them out. Macker had shinned down the back drain pipe and abandoned them. That's what bothered him, he tried to picture Tricia again, calling him from the window, but he saw her instead, still calling, and shaking their mother who would never wake up, saw her face dawning in horror, shaking and calling.

Macker pulled himself together, he had been walking crooked, chest tight, choking back tears. He kept his head down. He never cried.

"I'm sick, I'm sick" he muttered, shaking his head fiercely. He wished he could find out where they had been taken.

Macker stopped, had to lean on a wall for a minute, then he glanced back and forth, continuing Northward through a deserted carpark and old flats, and past the occupied factories. Walking, half dazed..There was a cop car now! Macker turned into a little shop, his heart leaping, it was really chancy here on the edge of the CoOp. He peered into the darkness.

"Sorry son." the woman said, "We don't serve knackers in here."

He stared for a moment into the heavy lined face. His mother had been genuinely sick, and his Da had only mockery left to give her. She was to blame, she had ruined him, a half traveller outcast by both sides. She had been fat, useless, old, Macker remembered it now, he had even joined in the torture. Now he turned and left the shop without speaking. Feeling dizzy again, head ringing, muttering, fists clenched. He was heading now for Little Agnes Street, where he knew of a loose side window, a quiet back room. Lots of boarded up houses in fact. It was further than he thought, it seemed much further, but he only had to get there. He would rest up, then go to the CoOp and get work on the farms. Yes, he would go to the country, it was summer!..But what was wrong with him? He was going to throw up now, no, he went on blindly and refusing to think, focussing his mind on that loose side window. Refusing to consider his sickness, and that old guilt and despair that conspired to destroy him. Young Macker McDonagh came at last to the corner and turned into Little Agnes Street.

He stopped there. Groaned. Opened his blurred eyes wide and closed them, as if to blot out what he saw.
The street was full of people. Banners hung right across. Children, dogs and cameramen milling about. Music playing thinly through loud speakers. And in the middle of it all stood one, two three, four cop vans! An Occupation, trouble. He would have to go back, really force himself now. Macker turned, felt his stomach rise and his vision going. Next thing he was doubled up at the corner, puking up a vile yellow mixture of whiskey and chips. As he retched he listened to a speaker, coming from some faraway compartment in his head.
"..we have taken over these good houses, to live and work in and to stop the stupid demolition plans which.."
Macker spat, grunted and spat again, lurched to a granite step and sat down, head between his knees. His eyes were pouring, a thin liquid dribbled between his teeth. "Just a few minutes" he was thinking "a few minutes rest and I'm off, oh Jayzus, I'm in fucking bits."
"Hey young fella." Macker heard it but he didn't move. "Hey young fella are you all right?"
Someone came down the steps and sat beside him. Macker uncovered his eyes and looked up. It was a young woman, with short red hair and blue eyes.
"Jayzus" she said, "It's Macker McDonagh, what the fuck happened to you?"
"I'm sick" he muttered, and spat, "I'm sick and I'm running." He shook his head, choking back another wave of nausea.
She put an arm round him, glanced across at the police.
"I wanted to kip in one of them gaffs."
"Yer OK Macker, come on inside. Them cops can't touch you in here, and you're in no fit state to be running."
Macker didn't move or reply, for the sympathy had dissolved him in tears. She was a strong woman but, and she took his arm and half dragged him up the steps.
Macker stumbled, peering through his black tangle of hair into a dark doorway.
"My name is Max" she said, "You're welcome here."

four james smith

James paused, glanced casually behind him, and hurried on. A tall figure in black, ducking his head slightly in deference to the freezing wind. Clutching under his arm a heavy plastic bag. He took a left turn into a narrow street of boarded up shops and occupied buildings. He glanced behind him again, the street here was still busy, though it was full dark, bicycles, lorries, carts and the armoured vans of the police. James was nervous, coming close now to the edge of the no go area, where the police dared not venture. But his nerves left no sign on his deep lined face, a sad expressionless face, which hinted only of long illness and life in prison. For prison had come hard to James Smith, formerly James Fitsroy-Smythe, first son of the millionaire industrialist, Sir Malcolm Fitsroy-Smythe. James had once been the rising star, the darling of the media, the brilliant young historian and economist, the flashy dresser and flashy talker. James Fitsroy-Smythe, heir to spectacular wealth, the young bourgeois taking a short cut to the very top.

James Smith turned up his coat collar against the bitter north wind, and allowed his scarred face to register a very slight smile, remembering back.

Back to his childhood, for he conceived of his life as a process, going along always with his family's plans for him, yet remaining aloof and calm. Observing the vicious power feuds around him with a somewhat detached and jaundiced eye. His was an old and respected family, successful and moving with the times, from colonial landed gentry to manipulators of money, goods and people, from factory and shop owners to corporate property managers. The young James had played his part, tongue in cheek, with all the confidence of the very rich. It was soon evident that he was a worthy heir, shrewd and intensely curious, he excelled in whatever he did. James, they said, was born to lead. He should have been a famous lawyer or politician, he could hardly have failed to extend the family's business empire. At the University, he had naturally been popular, for he was free with cash, and though cold and aloof he could put on a charming front. In debates he would cut up his opponents with icy precision, then smile and thank them. His path was firmly set, but within his private self doubts grew. For one thing he hated his father, who was pursuing classic economic theory..cut your workforce in times of recession, rationalise, cut out, and after that close up shop, mothball and reinvest overseas. James understood quite well that his own power and prestige rested firmly on the poverty and subjugation of others, that his family name was a curse in the vast new slums. Nothing had really changed in a hundred and fifty years, they were essentially the same landed gentry who had used mass starvation as a golden opportunity to create viable farm units. James saw quite clearly that it was necessary to starve or export people again. He understood the purpose of the police and army build-ups, the application of control theory, the desperate revival of religion, the apparatus of the secret police. But above all he was preoccupied, despite his supremely confident exterior, with his own lack of identity. For behind the family prestige, beneath the private self and the secret homosexual, beyond all the easy masks and games, he could find nothing...no meaning, no direction. As if he was so aloof that he didn't exist. James dug obsessively into himself, but found there only the certainty of annihilation, half seen half remembered glimpses of a terrified animal, crying in the dark. James concluded that he was nothing, no more than the sum of his memories and experience and, if they really existed, genetically inherited traits. He had tried to deny his education and upbringing, and detached himself, thinking that this made him a free agent. But he had reached the conclusion that free will itself is an illusion. He was trapped in what they had made him, he could not change, except perhaps gradually by living through a 'chosen' and different experience and situation. To remake himself, a haphazard and contradictory project, but one which haunted James Fitsroy-Smythe, during his lonely and egotistical ramblings, conducted over whiskey and sodas in his exclusive Fitswilliam apartment.

Left to himself James would never have acted. His life, though intellectually meaningless, was at least easy and pleasurable. It was the strange and nasty fate of his friend and lover Michael Dalton which broke the mould. A strange doomed friendship, based initially on the excitement of verbal battles. For despite his middle class origins and his many failings, Michael Dalton was irrevocably committed to a workers' Revolution. Spurning the lure of Party leadership and control, he and his friends had begun The Wildcats, a secret organisation dedicated through agitation, propaganda and sabotage, to the takeover of the workplace by the workers. They had in fact made some headway, due to disintegrating social conditions and the paralysis of the old Trade Unions, and were an early precursor of the Free Unions themselves. James Fitsroy-Smythe had found himself giving ground, for though he could parry with a hundred historical and economic objections, Dalton's vision was at least just and heroic. Dalton, moreover, was beautiful, his young brown skin, his open smile, the way he threw his fair hair back. Poised in the flickering firelight at the apartment, his eyes would grow moist, talking of ultimate failure and the certainty of war and death, and he seemed to James like nothing less than a young Greek God reborn.

A few short months, and Michael Dalton was gone, snatched with six comrades in dawn raids and charged with a #40,000 wages robbery, which James knew he could not have committed. James was distraught, and tried for the first time to use directly his inherited power and prestige. His father however was hostile. There was a brief court appearance. Dalton and his friends were produced, handcuffed and surrounded by armed police. For James it was the turning point, their eyes met in the packed courtroom, Dalton even managed a wink. But it was immediately obvious that they had been terribly beaten. Broken up and discarded like waste products. Police testified that they had resisted arrest. All six had signed detailed confessions. And waivers that they had not been mistreated. The hearing was over. There was no possibility of bail.

James went home to his own luxury cell, to his own private night of torment. It wasn't till the early hours that he began to suspect his father, that giant ego lurking always behind him. His suspicions grew. He was quite sure Sir Malcolm had had him watched. Michael Dalton was a terrorist and a queer, and as such a moral threat to the family name. Could it be possible that his father had had him framed?

Red eyed and exhausted, but strangely calm, James confronted Sir Malcolm next morning in his office suite. All his life James had never answered him back, and his father did not recognise his verbal skills, playing to his prejudice, then hooking and pulling. For though he denied the ultimate charge, Sir Malcolm had betrayed far too much knowledge of Dalton and what had happened to him. When he left that office block James knew, and his father knew that he knew, that Michael Dalton had been disposed of because he threatened the Fitsroy-Smythes.

James acted for himself at last, ironically, in anger and blind reaction. He cut all his family ties, left university and changed his name to James Smith. He did however keep the #7,000 in his personal account, and set about spending it, on the Defence Campaign, on parties, drink and drugs. He moved to a squatted house, and threw himself into the radical scene which flourished in the city at that time. Five months later he was arrested, with three others, in an abortive bomb attack on a police computer centre. He was sentenced eventually to six years, a light term, and served four.

James Smith allowed himself the beginnings of a grim smile, as he turned out of the cold wind into a narrower side street and clambered over a symbolic barricade. For he had succeeded in his quest for a new and freer identity, by freedom denied and experience forced upon him, and now chose to walk into a perilous situation, denying himself indefinitely for the greater freedom of all. At the next street light he saw a gang of kids, wearing black capes and high spiky hair. They were shouting, throwing shapes and swigging beer. James strode on, but he was uneasy, he was too well dressed for this area. As he approached they moved casually across the lane to block his path. At that moment the street lights went out. James stopped, heart leaping, poised to run.

"Oh shite."

"Who's got the light?"

A torch flashed up in his face. He was surrounded.

"What are you doin here mister?"

"Let's see in that bag."

"Search him then."

"I have an appointment with Bernard Maguire in Jude's Lane."

"What's your name?"

"James Smith."

"Ah yes you're expected."

"There's a load of papers in here."

"Okay pass through, its next on the left, third door."

James walked on into the dark, as loud mocking laughter echoed behind him. He found the turning, and a small, steel plated door. Groping for a bell he gripped a cord and pulled it. It was black dark, a bell tinkled far away.

James blinked at the bright pressure lamps as he entered the big main room. A big smiling fellow shambled over from the bar.

"So you're this James Smith then."

"I am yes."

"I'm Barney, we're sitting over there. This is James, this is Max, this is Jerry."

"How do you do."

"Would you like a drink then?"

"Well, do you have coffee?"

"Yeah, take a seat there" said Barney, "Coffee anyone else?"

"Yes for me and crisps." said Max.

James put down his bag of papers and sat straight, nervous and unsmiling at the wooden table.

"'Er, you found the place OK then?" said Jerry, "some people do have problems."

"Yes, I met some young people who directed me. The street lights have gone out as well."

"Twice a day they cut the power" said Max, "But it doesn't bother us, only for the workshops, and most of them have another source now."

There was a silence, till Barney returned with a tray of coffee, put it down and sat opposite James.

They poured coffee and the silence began again. "They're waiting for me to speak first" James thought, but just then Barney spoke, as he shuffled through some papers.

"Right, so" says he, "We're here to talk with you as a reception group. You've been recommended to us by some of our members in prison, plus we've made a few enquiries, um, how about if we explain the setup here and we'll see how you might fit in."

"No, no, we always let them speak first" Jerry broke in.

"Okay how about that."

James nodded, glancing up at the strange tired looking faces, the oil lamps smoking a bit, the posters, flags and banners. He spoke, adjusting his masklike face to the slightest of smiles.

"Well basically I'm a historian and an economist, that's what I'm good at, but I've a fair idea of what they're up to in sociology and psychology. Apart from that..." James paused a moment, "I did a bit of work for the Wildcats Defence Committee, and I got arrested on a rather ill considered job. As you know I was active inside, as far as possible, with some of your crowd and, well now I'm out, I want to help and I reckon I can."

The silence began again. Max looked bored. James began scratching his ear. Then Barney's puzzled look suddenly vanished.

"The Wildcats. Micky Dalton!" he cried, "Of course, you're Micky

Dalton's mate. You're James Fitsroy-Smythe!"

James' face remained immobile. But he was cursing himself for not admitting it himself.

"I was James Fitsroy-Smythe, I, well, I couldn't go through with it, I changed my name and disowned the lot of them." He looked up into Max's blank gaze.

"Of course!" Barney laughed, pounding the table, "Remember I was once thrown out of one of your debates.!"

James' mind flashed back five years, and he saw Barney again, heading a dirty looking group, disrupting the debate and yelling obscenities. He, as Chairman, had argued with them briefly, then had them ejected, forcibly, on the grounds that they weren't College members.

"Oh God yes" he said, "I'm so sorry I don't know what to say.

"Say nothing about it" said Barney, "times change and people change surely, I'm delighted to see you here so I am."

"I still don't get it" said Jerry. Then Max broke in suddenly.

"So you're from this super rich family and you fell out with them, why, and what happened then?"

"I quit everything. I was doing post grad work, lecturing a bit, they had me on company boards, they even had a marriage lined up for me, but, well..." James stopped, glanced at the three and back at the empty bar. Took a deep breath. "I'll tell you, privately, what happened, see all the time I never really believed in my life, well the turning point for me was Micky Dalton getting done..." he stopped again.

"He was a good friend of yours." said Max.

"Yes, yes yes he was...see Michael wasn't on that raid he was done for, because he was with me at the time, but I couldn't prove it. Some of his friends did do it all right. But the reason they took Michael was because my father and his cronies had had us watched, saw him as a threat to the family reputation, and asked their police friends to get rid of him.."

"Jeezus."

"What a fucking bastard!"

"Yeah well, that's how the break happened. I'm only telling you now to explain my motivation to you."

"Fair enough" said Barney, "You must have had a hard time."

"Yes I did rather, but I was such a spoiled brat before. At least now I'm doing something useful."

"Which brings you here."

"Which brings me, inevitably, here."

"How much do you know about what we're trying to do?"

"Just what I've heard and read, I know the story, the squatters' movement, the rent and mortgage strikes, the first CoOp Area, the linkup with the farm CoOps, the raids, the riots, the robberies er, the workshops and the defence groups and all than, then opening up all the new areas. It's revolutionary, extremely so in fact, but under the guise of something social and somehow harmless. Until the Free Unions sprouted up and the takeovers began, that's the main thing I think they..."

"You're wrong!" Max burst in, "You're making the whole thing sound mechanical like, like a fucking history book we're talking about people man, our struggle for a better way of life you don't even mention the basic things like the anarchist principles we fought for and which won out in the CoOps, or the Women's or the youth movements, the rejection of schools and authority the split in the church like the basic things which..."

"Whoa whoa Max give him a chance to finish" Jerry broke in.

"Give me a chance you mean, you would support him, you think the Free Unions are everything too just cos you're on the same power trip in them but you're wrong its not like, like organic anymore its just people jumping on the bandwagon, like this man, its all men trying to force a confrontation to wank their egos, you know its true, its too far too fast. What if they use the army tomorrow? Take back the factories in the country where we're weak, but our supply routes to the farms, then you'll see people turn back just as quick...its becoming a power game."

"OK OK you're right Max" Barney spoke up, "but its too late to stop it now. We've got to go for it all the way and compromise our principles as little as we can. The youth won't be held back anymore. In fact I can tell you now, I've quit working in the life education groups, I'm moving into defence work full time."

"What!" said Jerry, "You must be kidding."

"Jeezus Christ" Max flopped back in her chair, "now there's a sign of the times."

"That's by the way" said Barney, "James here has come to help us and we should hear him out, um, could you tell us briefly James what is it you'd like to do, we're all a bit exhausted here tonight." As he spoke the electric light bulb flashed on above them.

"Now there's a good omen for you" said Jerry, getting up to turn off the gas lamps.

"We can fix you up with a place to stay" said Max, "and there's plenty of work to be done."

"No no" said James. "I thank you, there's nothing I'd like more than to come and live and learn with you, but I can be more useful outside." James dropped his voice to a whisper, and glanced up the empty bar. "I'm offering you information" he said.

"How do you mean?"

"I mean as a spy." James had lifted his plastic bag onto the table, and now pulled out three heavy files.

"Since I got out or prison I've made a start. I've set up a Business Consultancy firm as a cover, with money from my sister, who naturally knows nothing of this, I've renewed some old contacts, and brought you here today some information I have already been able to collect, at very little risk to myself."

"Fucking brilliant." Barney was leafing through the first file. Max reached for the second.

"I've brought these files as proof of my good will. The first is details of firms in trouble and likely to close down soon. The second is a countrywide listing of empty properties, with various details and other information, and the third is a real piece of spying, it's a government file on the Free, including intelligence reports and contingency planning. It's slightly dated but..."

"This is unbelievable." Barney had leapt up and leaned across as if to embrace James.

"Hey Jerry take a look at this stuff."

"You're a wonder man, you walked through the streets with this stuff!"

"Yes, but that was a necessary risk, and the only real one."

"Amazing."

"Look it's time I left, a few details just..."

"Of course" Barney was waving his arms, "another meeting, you'll need contacts in our intelligence groups, you can..."

"No no, your intelligence is infiltrated."

"You think so?"

"I know so, all I need is a couple of places for letter drops. I'll run my own show and you'll be my contacts. Just the four of us OK?"

"Okay I suppose." said Jerry. "But how do we contact you?"

"Your contact for now is Professor Kearney, at the university. Just hand delivered letters, he's above suspicion..well, unless there's anything vitally important I'll be on my way." James had got up, leaned to shake hands, "Thanks a lot it was great to meet you all."

"No, thanks to you mate really we're most grateful. Are you sure you won't stay a bit?"

But James was already disappearing into the dark passage, and the bell tinkled as he closed the steel door behind him.

five **bastards**

My name is Patrick Grogan and I'm a bastard. My little brother Derrie is a bastard too, which means me Ma isn't married. My Ma Bernie done her best for us and I don't care a single token if she never got married. But I used to get a terrible slaggin at school. They would only call me a bastard if there was a gang of them, cos I'm a big young fella and I would go mad I would. When I lost me rat I would bash up anyone.

To tell you the truth I didn't even know what a bastard was. We used to be really poor and me an Derrie and me Ma lived in this flat it was a kip. I had to babysit Derrie every night nearly. Then Bernie would come home with loads of grub she robbed out of where she worked. I used to get really sick sometimes it was brutal. My Ma is okay and she knocked out a copper at the riots. I wasn't there but I'm let go next year when I'm at working school. We came to live here last year in the CoOp its great. We live in two houses in Little Agnes Street only its one house really cos there's doors inside. All the kids live upstairs and we have our own play room where I am now. There is me an Derrie, and there is Damo and Kathy and their little sister who is called Tricia. She's mad but I like her. Their brother Macker stays here too but he's grown up. Maybe they are bastards as well only their Ma is dead. Tricia seen her dead but she won't talk about it. There's a lot of bastards around here cos no one cares about getting married. The little kids are Derrie and Tricia and Tommy. His Ma is Max and he's a bastard too but his Da is Barney. There's a load of grown ups here too and they always shout at us to keep quiet. Only they make more noise when they do be drunk at night. The grown ups are Max and Barney and Maggie and Jerry and Josie and my Ma Bernie. I think there is more. The best of all is Josie she likes to play games with us. Next door there's a load of people making printing and stuff. The school here is great we only mess around and do projects. We have to do reading and writing but I like it. I'm the best writer in our group. Damo hates it sometimes he just runs outside. This place is called the Free but its not free really we have to do loads of things, cleaning stuff and all and we have to go to bed at ten o clock. You do get sweets for free all right but you only get one bag. The old fella in the shop ticks off your name when you get them. Liquorice is my favourite and I'm gonna be an Apache when I leave school. The Apaches all have horses and carts and cut their hair in the middle.

Me an Damo and Kathy have a secret house, we went there today when all the kids were playing den in the big yard. No one can find you there cos its all full up with junk and you have to crawl through a roll of carpet. Its a great house we have feasts there and all kinds of secrets. All Kathy did was dirty dares, we took off all our clothes. She has little tits and hair on her fanny, she's very interested in sex I'm not. I know all about it I even seen Barney and Maggie doin it once it was gas. Kathy dared me to do feelies all over. I'll do anything she'll do but it was her turn to go first she cheats. Anyway I can beat her at wrestling Damo learned me wrestling he's great at it.

The others have gone to the play but I can't go cos I'm sick. Its not fair. On Friday we're all going to the farms its great. We go in lorries in the middle of the night. There's loads of kids there and we go camping and swimming and all. Only thing is we have to do weeding. Steffo and Mark are coming to, they're in our school group but they're not bastards. This is my new secret book an I have to hide it good or Damo'll get it.

six christo

It was after seven by the time Christo Reilly left his office in the old transport works, and made his way slowly down the steep concrete steps, across the yard and out through the big iron gates. An early group of night shift workers passed by, greeting the old man with hostile glances, sniggers and sneers. The gatekeeper shouted an obscenity, in place of his usual nod and smile.

Christo walked on, ignoring them, his firm step and straight back belying his sixty two years. A big bluff smiling man, but a hard one. He had worked here for fifteen years, and done his time as a blacksmith, before rising to full time union official. And he prospered in that position, a man of transparent principle. The men knew and trusted him, the warm smile, the camaraderie, then the sudden flashing insight into people and situations. Over the years he had risen in the union, and his name had become a byword in the vast sprawling works. He had the makings of a politician, if he had wished for it, he had that knack of conveying to everyone that each was somehow noticed and special to him. Christo had become something of a father figure, to the people of those tight little estates, which surrounded the industrial area, and stretched endlessly into the former country-side beyond.

The management too had come to like and respect Christo Reilly. For after the displays of power and the fiery rhetoric he would always bring the two sides to a workable compromise. He had become an important cog in the institution, and he revelled in the position. For in truth there had been a little leeway here, throughout and even after the good years, in the age old battle between capital and labour. We were a public company after all, doing an essential service. Trains and buses there had to be, but there was no final exact way of assessing what they should cost. The great old works was a world unto itself, still abiding by the old demarcation, seniority and work rules and respect for the trades. A job in the works had always been considered a lifer, so that when parts of it closed down, there was only tighter competition for jobs. And as wages effectively fell, again and again, people still scrambled to get their sons into jobs or apprenticeships. The rest of the economy might go, but we believed the works would remain.

By the time he reached his middle fifties Christo had become a nationally known figure, game for anything, sound as a bell. He was called in to help negotiate complex disputes all over the country. The buses, the electricity workers, the lorry drivers, the postmen. But times had changed, irrevocably, as the private sector began to collapse, and the State itself tottered towards bankruptcy. Christo was soon asked to do the impossible, as the industrial workforce was halved... a long line of redundancy deals, speed ups, productivity agreements. We struck at last, and lost, and took voluntary wage cuts. And struck and lost again and the power of the union was broken. Christo and his colleagues remained, but even had to be paid by the State.

Christo Reilly stayed put, however, working against the tide, and still respected. Families who had one member working could survive, pooling the diminished wages with the pittance of the dole. The people had flocked into the cities and the population had surged, poverty had been all but forgotten in the brief decades of the bloom. Now the foreign factories closed, one by one, and it was only the spreading Co-Ops which saved many people from utter penury. Soon there was no profits, no investment, no resources, no markets, the only booming business was making arms for war, the vicious circle went around the world, and back. It was Christo himself who negotiated the deal, whereby the Co-Ops took over the redundant North West Works and leased the plant there. He had lost credibility on that deal, for they had moved in and never paid a penny for rent or hire. Yet they had set up an apparently thriving business, repairing and adapting their fleet of alcohol powered lorries, branching into factory and farm machinery repairs, scrap metal and workshops of every description. It was economic nonsense of course, yet still they expanded, for they offered little or no protection. Christo disliked them, this horde of new tinkers, the place had become a warren, whole families even lived there, amongst the great piles of scrap metal, wood and tyres. They took what was not theirs and there was not place for the likes of Christo and their scheme. Yet their ideas caught rapidly, as the new slums faced total destitution, two of his own family joined up, in fact this illegal economy must now be the biggest employer in the area.

For Christo and the union these last years had been a growing nightmare, as the screws tightened and his power faded away. The Works had been his life, and bureaucratic infighting his breath. And now the Free Union, mushrooming suddenly within the works itself. Demanding the impossible, trebled wages! Refusing negotiation, building up to a strike, and putting enormous pressure on Christo to come up with the goods. Cowboys, extremists, Christo had determined to fight them all the way. So that today, as always, he carried a briefcase of papers on his walk home, down the potholed streets and between the decrepit blocks of flats. And not a gurrier nor a hooligan would touch him, for he was Christo Reilly and they all knew it

He had never believed the management would betray him. Would they abandon the railways altogether? Would they throw away generations of laboriously acquired and jealously guarded skills? Would they really throw out men of 30 years service without a pension, and only a few months of pay?

Yet today the final blow has fallen. The Works and nearly all the rail lines will close. The logic of capita has caught up with us at last.

Christo Reilly walked straight, as always, but his step was not quite firm, and him mind was reeling. Something had snapped, deep inside him, when he opened and read the hand delivered letter. He had not reacted, just sat all afternoon at his desk, smoking and gazing out his filthy cracked windows at the yards beyond. It was left to his colleague, Jim Duffy, to get the last ditch redundancy campaign underway.

Christo was shocked, and in truth he was afraid, for the first time afraid and ashamed to face the workers.

"They can't do it" he muttered again, as he walked through the yard of paint scrawled block of flats. He just wanted to get home. It wasn't far now. But there, beside the piles of rotting garbage, stood three angry looking young men.

"Hey here comes the old lap dog himself."

"Hey Reilly you bastard, where are your promises now?"

Christo walked ahead, ignoring them, then one of them moved suddenly, bounding across to block his path. Christo tried to walk around him, but he found himself pushed staggering back. An old man, tensing himself to fight, calling all his old strength for this new threat, trying to banish his own dazed exhaustion and aching back.

"Too high and mighty to talk to us now are you?"

"No no" he blurted "I'm really sorry I never thought they'd do it."

"You knew" the man's face twisted in a snarl "you'll get your pension all right you scabby bastard."

The other two had wandered across, hands in pockets, and a crowd of kids came running.

"Ah leave the old wanker alone" said one of the men.

"I will fucking not! That man is a two faced fucking gombeen scab!" As the shouting began the children moved closer. Suddenly one darted forward. Grabbed and twisted the briefcase from Christo's had. Was off, dodging.

"Hey give that back" Christo ran a few awkward steps, white hair flying, then stopped, suddenly dizzy, and had to bend over, head in hands.

One of the young men held his arm.

"I'll get it back for you now, hey Gaybo, Frances, get the bag and bring it back here!"

"Are you all right, Christo, Christo?"

"Is he hurt?"

Christo said nothing, then heaved himself straight, tears streaming and pushed his way, arms waving, out of the little crowd. Walked quickly, back straight, towards his home.

Coming to the little gate a memory struck him, from half a century back. A smaller kid had beaten him up and he had run home crying. The same helpless shame, helpless fury.

He grimaced, laughed a little through his tears, and felt in his jacket for the front door key, hoping to avoid Pauline in the kitchen. But she must have been watching for him, the door opened.

"Christo. What happened to you?"

He was going to go past her, brush the old woman aside. Then he embraced her, suppressing a great shuddering sob.

"They're closing the Works" he said "An the kids robbed me bag."

Old Christo managed to get himself through to his study, and slumped down heavily at his desk, where he supped the strong sweet tea that Pauline brought him. Slowly his senses returned. The briefcase arrived, intact, at the doorstep as he expected, and he took out the letter and read it again. Warily, looking for an angle, like the old campaigner he was. There must be a way to fight on. He would negotiate redundancies, of course, that was his duty, but no, he thought, even this chore would be denied him. For now the Free

Union would have their day. The pittance of redundancy payments could not defuse it. The workers would no longer be divided. No, they would call one of their assemblies, they would occupy the Works, in league with the Co-Op gangsters. The place was worth millions, even as scrap at today's prices. The police might have to attack, God knows what would happen then!

Christo was coming out of his shock, his thinking coming clear, and his conclusions hard and logical. He was out of the fight, and his kind of union was dead. Both sides would blame him, of course. A convenient old scapegoat, impotent, powerless!
Yet still his mind was racing. He wanted to fight!.

A low knock came to the door, it was his wife, smiling but worried.
"Sasha's here to see you. I said you weren't well but she says it's important."
Sasha was his favourite grand daughter, an unlikely, almost flirting friendship had grown up between them these last years. He always tried to keep in touch with youth, and he found her quick, sharp and sympathetic..
"Thanks, you can send her in, I need a bit of cheering up."
Sasha walked in without knocking, Christo's head lifted at the sound of her voice, the sight of her long black hair and her young body in her bright blue overalls.
"Yes thanks Granny" she was saying "But won't you come and join us?"
Christo half lifted himself as she came in.
"Siddown pardner" she said a hand in his white hair, then peering into the watery blue eyes, "You survived, so."
"Of course" Christo grinned slyly "But what brings you here so fast, you're a bit early for the wake."
"Very funny" Sasha sat down on the floor "You're too suspicious by far, but it happens you're partly right. I have a job offer for you, from the Free..But I was coming round anyway, everyone's ragin over what happened."
Christo groaned, turning his head away.
"They got to you too then " he said at last.
"C'mon Grandpa, you know I was always in with them, the Co-Op not the Union."
"Same difference" he said, looking down. "A crowd of bleedin hooligans."
The low knock came again. There was a tense silence, as Pauline brought in more tea, and cake.
"Don't go away" said Sasha, rolling to her feet.

"No, no, I've got things to do in the kitchen" the old woman backed out, pulling the door closed behind her.

"The way you treat that woman is disgraceful."

There was a long pause.

"You can't teach an old horse to jump hoops" he said at last. Silence again, then Sasha broke into a smile, kissed him on the cheek, and began to pour herself tea.

"Fair enough Christo" she said "It's your own decision. You were always the smart guy, so I'm sure you see the situation."

She put down her tea cup and continued, in a low, angry voice.

"You're washed up granpa, kaput! Your union is smashed, and now they propose to crucify you. After twenty five years of pacifying their workers for them! You got no choices man...you gonna play dead? You want to sit around and dig your garden and pet your grand children and, and die of fucking boredom." She stopped, face flushed, her voice had risen to a shout.

Christo was calm now, his mind running ahead. He knew this game backwards after all..play for time, hide your weak points..only this time the negotiating issue was himself. He waited till Sasha sat down.

"I had thought about the garden, its in a bad state" he said.

Sasha laughed. Rolled over on the floor.

"That's fine then, you're afraid to fight back. Grand, so."

"I couldn't say if I'll fight or not" he replied "Till I hear all of your proposition."

"Okay here we go. The offer is this, two in fact. Number one, part time work training young people."

"What! In what? I'm redundant for christ's sake!"

"You're a blacksmith."

"I haven't been a blacksmith for twenty years."

"It's basic skills, no problem to you. Number two, you're invited to work with us, organising the takeover. We need your knowledge of the Works. You'd have to change your ideas but, we work in teams, no power structure, no leaders, no fucking patriarchy!"

There was a silence. Sasha picked up the tea cup again.

"If you want time to decide."

"No, no" said Christo "I want more information. You say takeover, what takeover? I mean, I figured they would occupy the place, rob what they could for scrap, if they could get away with it.."

"You're a year out of date, Daddio."

"What then, what can you do with a redundant rail and bus works?"

"Between you and me" Sasha winked "Cross your heart and hope to die."

"Okay but" Christo was smiling despite himself "But I'll be dead soon enough at any road."

"Well if things work out with the rail workers as planned, we'll be taking over the whole lot, the lines, the rolling stock, the engines, the stations..Why there's even talk of extending, opening disused lines, bringing back steam, the works!"

"You're joking, they can't do that."

"The rail workers want it. In fact this Works closure threat couldn't have been timed much better for us."

"But it's ridiculous, the cost..."

"It's happening Christo. The country's going bankrupt. They can't even pay the interest on their loans anymore."

"But the police, the army, they'll stop you."
Sasha laughed.

"Maybe they will alright, but the pigs are scared shite of us now, and the army", she shrugged her shoulders, "the Free are in the army too you know."

"But how can it work, really, the railways lose millions every year."

"I told you, we're working on a goods economy, its needs and priorities, no capital required just the decision of the assemblies, the free distribution of surplus. No loans, no banks, no parasites and politicians strangling us. Course we lack resources, oil, steel coal, I hear you say. So we have to trade for some things, we're working on that, the Free are in other countries too you know. And its amazing what you can find in the meantime."

"Or take over."

"Right enough, there's warehouses packed full of essential goods in this town, only no one but the rich have money to buy."

"Of course there are" Christo leaned forward, pouring more tea "I didn't realise the conspiracy had gone so far."

"Maybe you didn't really want to know" Sasha paused for thought. "Anyway, it's up to yourself, our proposition stands. You've always seen youself as working for the people of this area, you could have been a big union Boss downtown. That stands to your credit. Now if you want to fight on you just got to swallow your pride. We're organising ourselves now, but we still do need you. No one knows the Works better they say."

Christo Reilly paused to survey his options. But he found none. The good negotiator, he thought, knows when to submit tactically, and attack on completely different ground.

"Okay" he said quietly at last "I'll work with you."
Sasha had rolled onto her feet and was hugging the old man, slapping his back.

"Right then that's settled. The Works Assembly is tomorrow morning at ten in the old canteen. You can speak, if you like, as an ordinary worker of course."

Christo nodded, his spirits rising, as various possibilities flashed into his mind.

"And the takeover begins immediately after?"

Sasha nodded.

"With or without the rail workers, who have their meeting tonight."

Christo shrugged his shoulders.

"It does make a sort of sense to me I suppose" then he laughed out loud "I will speak, of course I'll fucking speak, and I'll support the takeover. Those bastards will regret the day they double crossed us!"

"Right then" said Sasha again "There's fighting talk now. Listen I have to go I'm supposed to be at two other meetings. Oh, can I use your phone?"

"Go ahead" Christo leaned back and watched, as she plucked the receiver and dialled. She got through fast.

"Hello Barreler?..yes that okay he's with us and he'll speak in favour tomorrow..yes of course, I told you he would..right, see yuh then."

"You know something" said Christo "You're a terrible bleedin manipulator."

"Runs in the family. Listen, you work on your speech, I'll see you at your office in the morning, and go to the meeting with you."

"That's not really necessary."

"No, but I'd like to anyhow."

"Fair enough" said Christo "Well I suppose we'll have good crack anyway."

"Right, see you then. No don't get up. I can find my way out" and the door banged closed behind her.

seven the free

Jerry stood up, calm as usual, and surveyed the scene in the big, low, dimly lit basement. There were about a hundred men there, in gangs and smaller groups, just a few women. The air was thick with cigarette smoke and loud excited talk. Great brawny men and little wiry ones, clad in boots and big black shoulder padded jackets. Young fresh faces, faces lined and balding, and faces old already, old with alcohol and frustration and hard labour. And lots of fierce faces, fists banging on wooden tables.

Jerry was thinking fast, he was brilliant at coordinating these meetings, but it was a precarious business. He planned to start it off with the concrete proposals, so that common needs could come before the grudges, jealousies and feuds which could plunge the proceedings into uproar. This must not happen now, he was thinking, this was the most vitally urgent meeting yet. Jerry raised his hands and clapped them together loudly.

"Are you right there lads, we better get moving" he shouted, "can we close the doors now, and can you all pull your chairs forward, you fellas there's no use sitting back there no one will hear you."

There was a loud scraping and dragging of chairs as Jerry went on, shouting.

"Okay my name is Jerry from the North East CoOp here and we're after calling these meetings. There's new delegations here since last time so I'll just point them out so as we know where we stand, like, as I say, we're the CoOp group." He glanced down at Frances, Maggie and Peter, "this here's the dockers and the warehousemen and they have some very important proposals for us, then these boys are from the power station, you're the railwaymen, right, the cement workers, yes, men from the oil depots, a delegation from the transport workers, er, the free lorry drivers union, that's Pat and the observers from North West, down the back, that's our security so mind your manners, and you can all mind your mouths as well. This is a private and secret meeting and we have no media here. That's nearly it, these fellows are from various smaller factories and yards and um, on my left is James Smith and his mates from a business consultancy firm, believe it or not, and they have a very fascinating report for us." The big room had gradually gone silent except for furious whispering, as Jerry yelled and waved his arms.

"So I'm about ready to sit down now. We suggest that the Dockers' Free should speak first, then James Smith, since they have the urgent proposals as you know, then we go round this way to hear the groups in turn, only those standing will speak, you'll all get your chance later .... Oh yes we plan to break for a half hour at ten and, could someone open the back window the smoke is terrible here. This is a closed door meeting we'll have to decide later what to tell the media. Right! That's my job done, the first speaker, you guessed it, is Micky O'Brien from the Dockers."

A small chubby man stood up, as Jerry sat down relieved amid scattered clapping. A small man but a great speaker. Used to open air meetings his voice fairly boomed and echoed round the cellar. He made clear brief points, the miserable wages, the lay-offs and redundancies, the eclipse and sell-out of the traditional Unions. O'Brien dwelt on the intimidation and vicious attacks by the police and the Special Branch, the machinations of the management, the flat rejection of their legitimate demands. The bitter Dock disputes were reaching a climax. Micky was up on his chair, fists shaking, as he came to the crunch of his speech. Tomorrow they had called a great Dock Assembly, they would strike to close down the whole port and occupy it as a Free Area..But first they asked for, nay they demanded, the full support in strike of all the unions in the port. And more than that, they were asking for the full material and armed support of the Free CoOps...

As the speech wound to a fever pitch, Jerry, Maggie and Peter were whispering loudly together. This was a shock. This was the first anyone had heard about armed help. The request would split the Free right down the middle, they could not agree to provoke the first use of arms. Then Jerry was back on his feet, as Micky O'Brien sat down, in a storm of clapping and stamping feet...

"Can we have a bit of silence here please, before the next speaker, I'm out of order here but we just want to know does this request for armed support have the backing of your Union?" Jerry had been landed in the middle, and for once he was furious. Micky was up again.

"Yes certainly we believe it has overwhelming support, it will be proposed at our Assembly tomorrow."

"So only when and if it is endorsed will it be an official democratic request."

"Well, er.." Micky's friends were nodding, "Yes of course, we're just telling you what to expect."

"Thank you, you can sit down now. The next speaker is James Smith, he's here as our guest so let's give him a big welcome."
James stood up, a tall black suited figure, out of place among these working people. His heavy lined face remained impassive, but the note book in his hand shook slightly. Here he was an outsider, his clothes, his upper class accent...But he wouldn't hide the fact, he was the best person to speak, and this was for him the culmination of months of hectic work.

"Thank you Jerry" he began, "we've come here to present a report on the Docks. Its a fairly detailed analysis of traffic over the last few years, with forecasts of what will happen if the docks are taken over permanently and amalgamated with the Free CoOps." As he spoke two men had opened suitcases and were distributing thick stapled volumes. "I'll just summarise our results, you'll have to read the report for details..By the start of last month we reckon 20% of all dock traffic was accounted for by the CoOps making them the largest single enterprise, functioning in effect as a trading company for foreign exchange and scarce raw materials. However, as you know a growing proportion of this trade is direct aid to and from the Free overseas. We expect all this traffic to keep growing quickly. If all the takeovers and projected schemes we know of actually happen then we could control 50% of trade within the next six months, as the CoOps are forced to do deals for essential materials. The next section is on the private traders, we've done a discreet survey and our sample suggests that nearly all locally based companies would still use the port, especially if they could avoid paying tax and duties. A lot of these firms may become part of the Free in any case, we have separate reports on this subject. The problem comes with the foreign firms, all the big companies, and especially the oil firms will pull out, and compensation may be the least of their demands, these are the big boys. Not that we can't get oil or anything else we can pay for. What we have is a political problem which brings us to the next section, page ninety seven. Fortunately we don't have missile bases here, and normally the big powers see us as just another bankrupt country. However if the whole country falls into our hands we blow our cover, as many groups have argued. It's not just our politics that are the problem, we'll be seen as reneging on our National Debt, which is their prime means of control and exploitation, and as beginning to bypass their monetary system entirely, which is a direct threat to their power, and a very bad example to the rest of the world. There is still some room for disguise, compromise and placation and we can only estimate possibilities, but let it be said, we reckon that if there is a revolution here there is an 80% chance of trade sanctions, which won't stop us, as well as a 40% chance of an actual naval blockade, which would, and maybe a 25% chance of a direct invasion, probably led by a proxy force of exiles and mercenaries. That's it folks, it's a chance. What we're saying is that a takeover won't destroy the port, but that it could lead very soon to a countrywide Free Area, which has some chance of survival, due to the present chaos and confusion amongst the imperialist powers. We are happy to answer questions, and to help in any way we can. Thank you all."

As James sat down, relieved, the whole place burst into applause and excited conversation. Several people tried to break in with questions, but Jerry was already announcing the next speaker, Matt Conlon from the power workers. It was not now recriminations, but sheer excitement which threatened to stop the meeting, as speaker after speaker offered the dockers full support, and announced their intentions to call emergency mass meetings for the following day. Jerry seemed calm as ever, intervening for quiet and announcing speakers, but he too was being caught up in the excitement as, before their eyes, the takeover of the entire port area became an urgent reality. By the time it came round to them the North East CoOp group had their reply ready. It was Maggie who got up,the first woman to speak, as she immediately pointed out. They too, she said, would call an Assembly for the following evening. They could promise material support, and could pass on the request for armed help. But it was very unlikely to be agreed, and even if it were, people would want to ask approval of all the other CoOps. But they would propose a compromise plan, that they barricade and fortify the entrances to the docks, and if the State forces did open fire, they would then offer arms in defence. Maggie finished by announcing further meetings, through the night, to sort out practical organisation.

It was 10.30 already and Jerry announced, amid loud booing, that there would be no beer, because of the need for clear heads. As he spoke the meeting was already breaking up into smaller groups, the security were issuing pass-outs, and queues were forming for sandwiches and tea. A big group of dockers had taken the centre of the floor and people were crowding in, to hear and to shout questions. Micky O'Brien had slipped away to where the North East CoOp were sitting.

"Hullo there boys and girls" says he, sitting on the corner of the table, "sorry to spring that request for guns on you'se."

"Stay here a minute" said Maggie, "I hope you realise what you're doing."

"Oh we do, we do, we have to stir everyone up now, before things get too heavy."

"Can I ask you this," said Jerry, "When exactly will this takeover start?" At that moment Frances came back to the table.

"The defence groups are calling a full alert," he said.

"Good" said Micky in a loud whisper, "because tomorrow is the day. If the Assembly agrees and we know they will, we'll be going straight ahead with our plans. You can keep this to yourselves but its obvious, if we wait a day we miss our chance. We're just hoping the cops and all don't move on us tonight."

"That's what we figured" said Maggie, "we've a list of things here to clear up."

"Fire ahead then."

"Right, first what about sealing off the port?"

"That's all organised, our own defence groups will close the three main roads and the rail links, with piles of containers. One road will be kept partly open. No, what we want from you is real support, lots of people, lots of media. We don't expect to get your full armed support, what we're hoping is that you'll move arms into the area in reserve, but it's mass popular support that we want."

"You've left it a bit late."

"We had no choice but to rely on your alarm system."

"Our problem is this," said Frances, "we want to help of course, and we need the docks, but we have to have our own Assembly and talk it out amongst ourselves first."

"Right, right, I was just going to say, our proposal is that you hold your meeting in the Docks, get everyone down there to our big warehouse. That way people can show mass support there and then, and we put the whole thing out on our media live. We think it might work, it's a question of time you see.."

Maggie was shaking her head.

"More and more manipulation" she said, as Peter arrived back with a tray of tea. After a whispered consultation Jerry replied.

"Okay we'll go along with that idea, but we'll have to consult other people, and there's going to be a lot of work involved."

"Oh yes Micky" it was Peter, "we've got the new bulletin here from Supplies Coordination. The usual lists of stuff we're seeking urgently and depots round the country where they have to go. Maybe you can supply us with some of this?"

He passed over a heavy file and Micky tapped it with his knuckles.

"Consider it done, if we have it you'll get it" Micky laughed. "Might as well get the lads working for a change."

Jerry was frowning.

"Maybe you'd better talk to yer man James Smith about that, like there's some people we don't want to push too far."

"Don't worry, we're hand in glove with James Smith."

"You are?"

"Sure thing, some of his crew are coming in to work with us, and we're taking over your old supply building as an outside HQ."

"You are?"

"Yep, we're moving fast now."

A tall, sharp nosed man was tapping Micky on the shoulder.

"Right you are Dessie" Micky went on, "listen I'll talk with you lot later..Oh yes!" he lowered his voice, "I'm supposed to ask you, our group's inside of the army, we don't have good contacts with them."

"I'll start that" said Maggie, "probably Defence are already onto them."

"Tell them to get a move on, there's going to be one hell of a row if this takeover comes off." Micky smiled, bowed slightly over his beer belly, and was off.

"Shit, shit, shit" said Jerry, "We're being railroaded all the way."

He could hardly be heard over the noise.

"Listen, I'm going upstairs, I've a rake of calls to make. You better get this meeting started again." Maggie glanced around, the low hall was milling with people, a man was setting up camera lights around the dockers.

"Get up Jerry, there's not even supposed to be reporters in here."

"Shit, what happened all the security?"

"Get up and do your thing Jerry, it's a bleeding madhouse in here."

"Hey Max, Max it's back that way!" Maggie was shouting and waving, in the middle of the excited angry mob. I turned back, still pushing Tommy, who was struggling to get out of the pram. We had come down to see this history making assembly in the docks, but we could hardly get in, it was like a fucking scrum so it was. Me and Maggie found the Creche at last and we dumped Tommy there. There was a gang of women giving out leaflets saying they shouldn't occupy the docks, that they were all macho morons

and it'd lead to civil war and so on. We were inclined to agree, but it had to
happen sooner or later. Back in the warehouse and it was packed tight.
They'd given out voting cards at the doors, we even got them, and they were
starting to collect them already. People were roaring an yelling and trying to
climb up on the stage, where they had this old codger Christo Reilly up
speaking, all sweet and reasonable, while the place got hotter and hotter, like
a bleedin pressure cooker I swear it. You could hardly hear old Christo, an
when he stopped there was a storm of noise, there was whole families there,
clappin an screaming. So they had to get Micky O'Brien up to cool it down.
Micky is their big fucking leader, with a gang of fellas around him, holding
up their arms for silence. The first thing struck me was they they were his
bodyguards. Was this some mini-Hitler we had thrown up? He was a little
fella all right, and he had to pull over the mike stand to talk quietly into it, an
everyone had to shut up just to hear him. He got us all sitting down, and the
cards collected, and things got moving, explanations and requests and
messages for various people. Then they were trying to divide up the whole
mass into groups of about three hundred, under various flags. Me and
Maggie sat and watched. To us this was a power play and it stank, but no,
Micky was no Hitler, though he was still the Leader, which made us sheep.
There was a big row goin on at that time, not so much in the Docks but in the
CoOps, a lot of people were against being dragged into a total confrontation
by this so called Free Union. Partly it was because we'd built ourselves up
and now we had something to lose, and partly it was true, it was the men
really, Barney included, all being pulled and swayed and led by the noise
and, it seemed to us, sliding willy nilly into the jaws of some great big war
machine.

Yes I did feel bitter, against those men with Micky on the stage. Yet they
looked embarrassed, hiding their hands now in their pockets, a bit
dishevelled, squinting at the crowd through the camera lights. They were
ordinary blokes, almost pathetic, yet they were throwing out, to the whole
world, this brilliant and desperate challenge.

Than Maggie was pointing, and there was a cheer as a man stood to read
out the result of the first vote. It was 90%, the strike would begin
immediately. People were upon their feet, leaping about,and we had to
stand too, as the unexpected second vote was announced. That was the clue
and the key, that second, black card, calling for a takeover by the Free
Unions and a merger with the CoOps system. When this was announced
they went crazy altogether, and I must admit me an Maggie were clappin and
huggin each other with the rest. It was like a Declaration of Freedom, it
must've taken five minutes to stop us cheering.

By then the defence groups had mostly left, bulldozing their way through the doors, and away off to close the roads. Then they were calling forward the big gangs and sending them out different doors. I heard a list read out...helping block the roads, occupying the offices, storming the Harbour Police station, preventing ships from leaving, guarding warehouses and machinery, touring the various factories...that's some of it I remember, they had it pretty well thought out.

We went with the third big crowd, out the side door we had come in. We were handed pink pass cards, and in the yard, heavy sticks. A bloke with a megaphone explained it. Then we were running, jogging really, towards the North entrance about a half mile away. The first part was just a mass trot, but as we got close we could see a lorry pulled across the road, and a traffic jam building up. Then this van load of police led by a Special Branch car came careering out of a side turning, just ahead of us. Away off towards the road block. Running together we screamed after them, some hurling their sticks at the fleeing van. Maggie had a stitch and dropped back, but I was having a great time. Laughing and running up at the front. Closer and closer. The cops were at the road block. Skipping the queue and hooting madly to get past. We were almost up on them. I thought I would see a fight. The Branch were out of their car, guns drawn. The coppers were about to abandon their van. But just then the lorry moved forward to let them slip past. We were right on them, two cops missed the van altogether and had to run like fuck. Sticks whistling past their ears.

We stopped there, panting, hands on knees, and the others all catching up, laughing and gasping and clapping each other's backs. There was Maggie, all freckles and her shock of red hair flying. Maggie my darling why did it have to be you! From the lorry a man was calling for us to link arms across the road. The cars had to go back, not protesting, hadn't they just seen the Law running for their lives!

There we stayed for about an hour. Back up at the railway bridge a huge crane was lifting containers from a queue of lorries, and beginning to swing them into position. They sealed up that bridge, containers on both sides three thigh and across the top. We had to head back then to pick up Tommy and help prepare for our own Assembly that evening. It was at the other gate further south that it was all happening, with all the bands and the cameras and later the human blockade and the army due to move in at dawn. If only I had known beforehand what would happen then.

It was a truly beautiful room, massive sparkling windows overlooking the Castle yard, huge marble fireplaces, ornate ceilings and massive blue and yellow glinting chandeliers. Around the polished mahogany table sat three

Generals, the Police Commissioner and lesser chiefs. But they were not concerned with beauty, ruffling their papers and talking in quick serious voices.

Among these military men sat Peter Kennedy, younger than the rest, but immaculate in his grey green uniform. He was an officer with an impressive record, and now an invaluable personal aide to the ageing General Mulcahy. There was only one thing out of place in that beautiful room, and only Peter knew of it, for Captain P. Kennedy was a spy.

At exactly five o'clock Lerriman arrived. Practically stomping into the room at the head of seven of his Cabinet. He had had a hard day, first more economic disaster, and then this ludicrous and dangerous business with the Docks. He would get to the bottom of it. He stayed standing, skipping all preliminaries.

"Right Commissioner, you're the one in the hot seat. How in God's name did you let this happen?"

"Yes Sir" the police chief cleared his throat. "At 11.00 am this morning an Assembly of all the Dockworkers and their families was held in a place called Mackenzies Warehouse near the North Wall. We had men there of course. These dockers are being led by a small group of known subversives who have set up a Free Union after the virtual demise of the MPGWU."

"Get to the point man, for Christ's sake."

"Well they were voting for another strike attempt, but a second voting card was handed out, to occupy the whole dock area. It was a trick. By the time we could respond it was too late. They have sealed all access with containers and trucks and made a big media spectacular of it. Right now they control the docks, the ships, the warehouses and the railways. Most of the factories are having mass meetings and joining in, and the North East CoOp are holding an Assembly in the Docks tonight. At this moment there is one road open to pass holders. But they can close it at a moment's notice. Traffic is now beginning to move in the port, they've obviously been making a lot of deals, but they are also committing wholesale robbery. Two convoys of lorries have already gone out into the CoOp controlled area."

The Commissioner stopped. Stared at his hands.

"This is crazy" Lerriman squeaked, "it's mad, it's ridiculous. Hundreds, thousands of people must have been in on this, and you say you knew nothing. You're implicated Commissioner! I can't believe what you're telling me."

"We did know of provisional plans. And, er, defence groups they call them." The top cop spread papers nervously on the table. "Here, we've been warning you about this particular Free Union for months now sir. But the fact remains that until this morning only a few people knew about this Takeover..."

At that moment Lerriman's fist hit the table with a bang, and a new sheet of paper slithered across the mahogany.

"And you were one of those few!" Lerriman shouted. "Do you deny that here is a copy of a letter, from the Special Branch to yourself, and delivered last night, warning you of the Takeover plan!?"

The chief of police went grey. Muttered incoherently at Bruton who was calmly lighting a cigarella.

"If we were to respond to every paranoid letter sent by the Special Branch we'd need the Gestapo to run the country."

"Paranoid? This is a major insurrection!! Do you know I have ambassadors going mad over this already. We'll be the laughing stock of the world.. We can't even get into our own port which is half.."

Lerriman stopped. Grasped his own head. Then he was off again.

"Negotiations" he snapped, "What is it they want?"

There was a silence.

"Flaherty!" he shouted, "Are you the Minister of Labour or am I in a fucking monkey house?"

"Yes well Sir, we're approaching them, but well, they've got what they want now."

"What do you mean you old fool, they must have demands."

"No Sir I'm sorry. The only room is on Customs Duties. That that's unlikely since, as the commissioner says, they're slipping goods out through their own area."

Lerriman cursed quietly through the next silence.

"Right then Commissioner. Before I fire you, what are your plans to recover the Docks?"

"Yes well we have been working on that", he stopped, then blurted on, "until now we haven't found a way, in fact its.."

"Why the fuck not? What's wrong man, you have thousands of men, armed trained. Go in and take it..Bruton, what does the Special Branch think, has the Commissioner lost his marbles?"

"Not entirely Sir, it will be difficult to get a big force in there all right, and we will have to clear away at least 5000 civilians first, before meeting their armed defence. The police are demoralised and infiltrated, in fact they wouldn't do it at all, while the Free are playing their pacifist game, hiding their arms and playing the whole thing live on their pirate media, so we can hardly suppress the facts. Now we could do the job all right, but our forces are too small. Mulcahy's your man now Sir."

"General Mulcahy" Lerriman was getting desperate, "Have you a plan to stop this rebellion?"

Mulcahy coughed before he spoke. A big man, overweight now and grown old. Still sharp and quick witted but plagued by high blood pressure and a nasty stomach condition. He felt his stomach flip now, as his name was called, and suppressed a grimace of pain.

"Yes Sir we can take the Docks. Our plans are not yet finalised, er, but basically we take the weakest point, and go through with tanks and bulldozers" he paused to belch. "Our commandos take all the key points, then we saturate the area, round up the subversives and cart them away."

Lerriman looked around him, it was far too simple. Everyone was looking down, except the smiling Special Branch chief, Bruton.

"You like that plan then, Bruton?"

He shrugged, still smiling.

"I'm not qualified to say, Sir, whether his old tanks will go through a pile of containers. But I know what they'll do to the thousands of idiots who want to stand in the way, and the result of that.."

"Oh yes" Mulcahy broke in, "I forgot to mention that we'll disperse any crowds with rubber bullets, tear gas, water cannon and warning shots. They'll have to move away."

Lerriman was still looking at Bruton, who raised an eyebrow and continued.

"The second major problem is infiltration, the Free have a strong foothold in the army now, and there are further difficulties. These people are well armed and they're no fools. Still I reckon Mulcahy's plan has a chance of success. These revolutionaries are getting far too cocky, er, well if you're giving the order chief, I'd like to send some of my boys along, for the crack so to speak."

Lerriman sat thinking for a long minute, while everyone waited.

"I don't see any other alternative, it's a grim choice we must face but, I mean, we have to suppress these people."

"Okay with me" said Bruton.

"If they get away with this they will get away with anything."

The others nodded, or didn't move at all.

"That's decided then, I want civilian casualties kept to a minimum. You can go along, Bruton, and liaise the police with the army. I want a military conference at eight o'clock. There's one more thing, Commissioner. I am relieving you of your post. You have done a good job until now but times have changed" he stopped. The police chief shot to his feet. Went to storm out. Then turned..

"Just one thing Lerriman, I think you make a big mistake to put police matters in the hands of a senile General and a sadistic maniac. Good day to you."

There was an embarrassed silence, then Lerriman spoke.

"You really think you can handle this Mulcahy, give us some details now."

"Yes well, as I say, we go straight in by surprise. Through the South gate. At dawn tomorrow morning if we can arrange it" he glanced at Peter Kennedy and the Generals. "Yes, at dawn we'll set up a little diversion, send some boatloads of soldiers down the North Wall."

Lerriman's eyes gleamed.

"At dawn, yes that sounds much more like it, maybe we will even catch them sleeping."

Bruton laughed loudly as the meeting ended.

It was the same big square warehouse, full to the corners and buzzing with life, but we had had a whole afternoon to transform it. The scaffold stage of the Dockers had been dismantled, and part of it reassembled in the middle of the floor. Lights and speakers had been put in, and areas partitioned with canvas. Two lorryloads of carpets had been found, delivered and laid out, dividing the floor into big irregular squares of colour. Banners and flags were draped and hung down from the roof girders. Outside big tents had sprung up around the railway sidings, and people were milling in and out and queueing for food. People everywhere, gangs of kids in weird costumes and multicoloured hair. Beyond the marquees crowds of little tents and camp fires flaring in the fading light, across the tracks another warehouse and behind that a stage and bands playing. Summer was coming again, and we needed no excuse to start a festival.

Maggie, Max and Josie were threading their way among the huge crowds sitting and squatting on the bright new carpets. They were giving out leaflets from the Women's Collective, smiling and arguing earnestly, leaflets urging that we avoid a direct confrontation with the State. But their leaflets were already out of date, the rumour had come first, then it ws announced at the start of the Assembly...that the Army planned to attack the docks at dawn. New posters and leaflets were going out already..JOIN THE BLOCKADE..and..WOULD YOU SHOOT YOUR MOTHER?..and were being plastered all over the city and even inside the army barracks. The Free Radios were reporting almost nothing else and calling for an immediate General Strike. The State media were still trying to ignore the rumour.

At the North East Assembly in the Docks the routine business had been rushed through and now there was a break before the main debate. There were three main proposals, the first, to take up arms immediately in defence of the Free Docks, the second, to make ready with weapons but only to use them if the army attacked, and the third, which most favoured it seemed, to rely on the human blockade already growing at the gates, and to plead with the soldiers to desert and refuse to fire.

The great warehouse was humming with excitement, queues of people from various groups were arguing for a chance to speak. More news was announced, people were marching into the city from the suburbs in growing crowds. A riot situation was developing outside the Central Post Office. It was announced that the Assembly was being relayed live around the country, and that speakers would be restricted to five minutes. The meeting was ready to commence.

Macker was exhilarated. Living on his nerves. Rushing with his media group from one job to the next. Volunteering for work in his time off. He was carried along with it, the Takeover, the Assembly, the human blockade, the mass of people in action. Macker felt, for those few days, like an immortal..

Macker stood now outside the South Gate, waiting to cut in with a live interview that he, Maurice and French Jenny had set up. Listening to the Assembly on the radio. It was exciting, they knew that half the city must be listening in, and the station was being relayed through all the Free Radios, and on the growing overseas network. Macker tried to relax, watching the big cranes at work, stark against the arclights, as they piled up containers all along the railway embankment. A loudspeaker system was being installed outside the gates. Great rolls of barbed wire were being unrolled all along the quays. They stood amongst a small determined crowd, already sitting in front of the barrier, though there was no danger at this time. Other press and camera people were flitting about in the unnatural black and white light.

Back at the Assembly an old man had been helped up to the microphone. He put on his shaking glasses and read from a piece of paper..

"My name is Patrick Daly and I'm seventy four years old. Me and my family all been in the CoOp from near the start, we done a lot of work building it up and I'm not boasting. I been a working man, I have seven children and eleven grandchildren. None of us want to see what we built up ruined, and nobody wants a war less than me. But I seen all this coming for a long long time. I seen us reduced to begging and I seen the coppers raiding, I seen them destroying the houses and I seen the prisons filled up to bursting. I have seen the youth, pulling at their bonds and longing to be free. Now here tonight I seen Christo Reilly, and I seen Micky O'Brien speaking for the workers, and I know one thing sure, that no since the time of big Jim himself have we been so strong! To me all you'se here are like my own family, and I can tell you this, whether we win or lose, if we don't fight them now we will never have a better chance again!"

As the old man finished, and the Assembly erupted again in cheering and clapping, Maurice received the go-ahead, the link was made, and Macker began his interview.

"Here we are back at the South Dock gate, standing under the shadow of the huge barricade of containers. We have here Brian from the Defence Groups, Brian, can you tell us what is planned to happen here if the army arrive at dawn as we expect?"

"Yes, well its not finally decided how we will resist them, that's up to the Assembly, and we should know the result in an hour's time. But certainly we're closing the roads, this is the last route and it will be sealed an hour before they arrive, and all these people here and we know thousands and thousands more want to make a blockade here in front of the gates. We advise all those coming to wear heavy clothing and crash helmets. We're expecting to receive a lorryload of gas masks soon, but that won't be enough, so bring your own if you have such a thing, and lemon juice, it neutralises the gas."

"You expect a gas attack then?"

"Yes, our information is that they plan to use tear gas and water cannons and warning shots. But I don't think they can clear us that way, especially if this breeze keeps up we needn't worry too much about gas."

"So what will happen then?"

"Well we're hoping the soldiers will refuse to fire, and they'll just have to give up. Certainly they won't move us easily, we're a very determined people now..I myself for instance am a docker, but I haven't had a day's work this year. Now at last we're getting the Docks moving again. If the government, or the rich capitalists who control them want to stop us, they'll have to kill and injure thousands of innocent working people to do it."

"Thank you Brian Connor. We will be back here live later on, but I hand you back now to the Assembly."

Maurice had cut the link and Macker was clapping Brian around the shoulders.

"Great stuff" he said, "that's fucking perfect."

Back at the Assembly Barney Maguire had just begun speaking for the

Defence Coordination. A short speech, but one he'd spent hours working on, fighting back sleep the previous night. Now the situation had changed drastically and he had had to change it all again. Barney seldom spoke at meetings, but he was a well known figure, he had been in the Free CoOps from the beginning, hadn't he written a book on the ideas of the Free. He spoke now in a low, warm, urgent voice, appealing for calm and careful thought. It would be completely wrong to take up arms, as the Dockers sought, to break a basic principle without first consulting all the CoOps and unions of the movement. He appealed to all, however, to prepare for an almost certain civil war. Let the army take the docks, if they insisted on a massacre, and let them be responsible for that war. All must be prepared, the factories, the supply routes, the warehouses, the CoOps, the farms, all could be attacked. He appealed to the people to stand by their beliefs and not to vote rashly out of time. Still he spoke quietly, with sudden bursts of anger, against the police and army chiefs, the fascists, the government, the international media, and finishing with an appeal to the soldiers, anyone listening over the radios..They could not, they must not open fire on their own people. Anyone deserting would be given a full place in the CoOps..by now the stewards were clamouring for time, and Barney ended with a last appeal, to all to remain calm and free, rejecting all authority, and standing together, whatever happened. Barney left the stage, amid applause that went on and on.

In the city centre people had been gathering, first in small groups, since early evening, when the rumours of an army attack on the occupied docks began. Soon the crowds spilled off the pavements, as shift workers responded to the first calls for a General Strike. By nine o'clock traffic was at a standstill. A large section of the crowd set out to march on the Prime Minister's suburban residence. They were stopped by riot police, and split into smaller groups who began a rampage, smashing, looting and attacking the police. Further crowds, marching spontaneously into the city, got caught up in the fighting, which spread out in all directions. Later that night the police were reduced to defending their stations, embassies and government buildings.

Midnight and everything is decided. A black dark night, but over the port area a few stars are struggling out. In the big warehouse people are unrolling sleeping bags, many are sleeping already. Outside, beyond the big tents, circles of people are sitting and squatting round camp fires. At one of these sits Macker McDonagh with his young brother and sisters. He is playing a guitar, repeating a low mournful tune. Half a mile across the railway sidings the concert is still in full swing. The young crowd have built a huge fire, dragging in railway sleepers and giant tractor tyres. At their makeshift stages the frenetic music continues till the dawn, in a storm of dancing coloured light and sound.

Barney sat at a desk, shielding his tired eyes from the neon striplights. Now chewing on his biro, now holding his head in hands, now tugging at his long greasy hair. He had spoken too well at the Assembly..they had asked him to make the appeal to the army when they arrived, they had asked Micky O'Brien first but he had refused. Barney kept trying to picture the situation, but however he tried he couldn't see the soldiers refusing orders, never mind throwing down their guns. He felt responsible..Of course he was partly responsible, and Max had been right passionately opposing the blockade, this was no time for stupid pacifist stunts and the making of martyrs. Barney was sitting upstairs in the new Dock Defence HQ, peering about the office floor he couldn't even spot anyone he knew. He was deadly tired, again he tried to picture the scene, as if by an effort of will he might yet stop the attack. Perhaps they wouldn't come, they would cancel the Operation, having lost surprise. But no, Barney realised, if the State had decided on stupid brute force they wouldn't back down no, there were too many egos involved, and again that feeling of guilty horror began to creep over him. Earlier he had been confident, the whole idea of the human blockade had crept up on him, he had been sure and arrogant and he had told Max to fuck off with her presentiments of disaster. But she had not been wrong before!
"Oh shit I can't do it" - he said out loud. He must find someone else to make this appeal. Yes he was overtired, unreliable...

It was after two o'clock when Maggie finished work and made her way through the dark wide yards to the new defence building. Lorries were still trundling about, and teams of people were rolling out barbed wire right down to the water's edge. Dark figures, armed and helmeted greeted her and hurried by..She entered the brilliantly lit office building, flashing her CoOp pass. She was looking for Barney, guessing that he would be tormenting himself now, he mustn't fuck up the appeal! She found him, sweating and waxen faced, at a desk on the third floor.
"Howaya goin there Barney?" she yelled across the space.
Barney turned and saw her, her red hair and freckles, shambling through the office chairs. To Max he was wildly attracted and repulsed, but Maggie he

just loved.

"Maggie! It's great you came up!"

"What are you doin working at this time?"

"Oh Jeezus I'm trying to write this fucking speech but I can't do it Maggie I honestly can't..Mickey will have to speak."

Maggie had found a revolving chair and was spinning around.

"Course you can do it, sure its an appeal not a speech. And its much better if Micky doesn't do it, he's too much of a leader already. You don't even have to write it Barney, just say what you said today."

"I know, I know, but I'm sure they'll open fire. And Max has a premonition. The people expect me to talk them out of it but I can't, honestly I can't do it I'm fucked.."

"Jayzus Barney you got the rattlers, come on now for some coffee and get some kip."

Maggie stood up.

"I'll tell you what Barney, I'll come along with you, and if you dry up I'll do the stupid appeal myself."

"You're not going out there as well?"

"We're all going out, Max is coming too. Its nothing to do with you Barney, we're doing it anyway and its not your fault you're just bleedin paranoid man..c'mon lets get out of this fucking office."

Barney followed her down the stairs and over to the tents, where they drank tea, and he followed her to a little tent and fell asleep beside her, though he swore he couldn't.

4.00 a.m. Thursday, and the first co-ordinated army movements had begun, with three major convoys converging south of the riot torn city. Two thousand policemen had already arrived from all over the country and were already at work, blocking off and securing the route to the Docks, which ran mainly through former middle class areas. The cordon was breached at many points by hundreds of molotov, throwing youth, but the police drove them back with the gas, dogs and baton charges, leap frogging ahead of the slow moving army convoy. At a quarter past four every boat and ship in the harbour began blowing its horn.

Danny Dwyer heard the distant horns begin, he saw rioting and destruction on both sides of their route. He was sitting at the back of an army truck. Sitting with twenty others fighting back panic. Plucking up courage to words.

"Hey you fellas" he shouted at last "I hope none of you are opening fire this morning."

"Right Dwyer" it was the officer, "one more word and you're under arrest."

"Go right ahead sir, but there's six of us here in this truck. Anyone firing on our women and kids will get shot down from behind."

"That's it Dwyer. Court martial, you're under arrest."

There was a rising murmur of mutiny.

"Arrest him and you can arrest me too."

"You can fuck off Sir, if you arrest him."

"Leave him alone."

The officer was cursing, and lurching about the swaying truck. But eventually he sat down.

"Maybe we won't have to fire anyway" he muttered to himself.

In fact Danny Dwyer was not in the Free, nor did he know of any other dissenters in the truck. But he had got the whispers, seen the posters and leaflets. What had enraged him was a thick stapled list that had been passed round the night before, entitled ... "List No. 1 of soldier's relatives standing with the Free" scanning it A to Z he had seen at least forty Dwyers on that list.

The lorry trundled on, bumping over bricks and blocks and glass and failed barricades. Skirting the South East of the troubled city.

Maggie was dozing off herself. But she heard the horns and hooters at once. She was up, shaking Barney in the little tent. Barney woke. Heard the noise. Saw flames, and was struggling for the tent flap. Outside people were slowly emerging from bags and tents. Someone had piled the camp fire high, flames leaping crackling.

"Wait Barney! Put your boots on you big eegit."

Maggie and Barney joined in the sleepy crowds, spilling out of the tents and the big warehouse. To the East the sky was lightening behind the black cranes, the wind was cold, but it could be a fine day.

People began to link arms, walking towards the arclights over the South Gate. Someone started an old CoOp song, and in a minute everyone was singing.

Macker, Maurice and Jenny hadn't slept at all. The radios were broadcasting all night, from camp fires, from the South Gate, from the riots and demonstrations in the city. They broadcast the singing, as the seemingly endless mass poured out of the narrow entrance between the containers and began sitting down on the wide road junction beyond. Macker was a centre of action, he didn't feel tired at all.

James Smith was up too. Sitting alone in his flat. Then rising and a pacing up and down. Sipping sweet tea and listening in to the Co-Op and police radios, and outside the dawn full of wailing sirens. Then he heard shouts and breaking glass. Flicked off the light and was at the window. He saw a dozen figures retreating down the street, ahead of a line of riot police. The army convoy was passing, by the sea, just a mile from where he lived.

Jerry, Bernie, Frances, Josie and Max stood together, arms linked, only five lines from the front, but maybe a hundred yards out from the gate. The whole intersection, the whole road North, was a solid mass of people, a gigantic choir singing together, Max sang along, had gone along, but she felt it was folly, and like all but the most unfeeling, felt a cold ball of fear rising in her stomach. Their helmets and sticks, and the gas masks slung around their necks, seemed to her no protection at all. Behind them the crowd had at last stopped emerging, and the tall cranes were swinging the last central containers into place .. There was no escape now. On one side, the river, behind them the barricade wall, on the other a mass of people, determined not to move. Ahead of them the enemy coming.

Maggie and Barney had made for the red Cortina, near the very front, where a Defence group, electricians and media were anxiously waiting. By now Barney's excitement and fear had wiped out his depression, fatigue and guilt. He took a slug of whiskey from one of the group, as another showed him how to wok the microphone.

"If they fire gas, jump in the car, it's sealed tight so you can go on talking."

"Okay okay" Barney was fumbling with his notes "Maggie here is helping me. She'll speak as well."

"That'll be fine" said the boy. "Try out a few words to get the feel of it when they stop singing."

"Just keep cool, we can only do our best" said Maggie.

Macker had spotted them from behind the car, where media and defence people were listening with headphones and scanners to their army and police radio channels.

"Hey Barney, Barney!" he yelled above the tumult of singing. The shaggy head turned. Macker was holding up both thumbs.

"Give 'em all you got!"

Barney nodded, pointing at his notes.

"Five minutes, five minutes" someone shouted.

As the verse ended, Barney spoke.

"Hello I'm Barney" he said, almost recoiling as he heard his own voice booming up an down the street, "I'm doing the appeal at this gate, and my friend Maggie here is helping me. First to repeat the advice from the Defence groups. If they fire gas we don't budge. Don't touch the grenades without gloves, if you catch hold of one put it in one of the water buckets. Or throw it back, the wind is blowing quite nicely away from us. If you haven't got a proper mask, hold your breath or breathe through a wet cloth. Their grenades only go for half a minute, and we hope they'll stop firing when we won't budge. If they bring up the watercannon, those up front hold up your shields, remember they only have a few of them and they empty in a couple of minutes...."

Barney was reading from a piece of paper, his voice echoing across the great crowd, from speakers set atop the barricade, and via the radio links, across the whole country.

Lerriman, the prime minister, was awake and fully dressed, with his private secretary in the study at his suburban residence. Now he slammed down the telephone down the telephone, red faced, eye bulging. Across the room Barrington was tapping helplessly at another phone.

"Now they've cut the fucking phones on us!"

Earlier in the night a fierce mob of rioters had penetrated almost to his front garden. Outflanking the police and charging down lanes and across gardens. He had been shocked, outraged and then openly terrified, as police fired in the air, and evil smelling gas seeped under the doors. Now, like everyone else, he turned in to the Free radios, suddenly hearing Barney's voice.

"First of all we'll appeal to them not to fire, they may shoot in the air but we'll ignore that. Then we'll be asking them to come over. Now it may happen there will be firing into the crowd, if they do that it'll be the Military Police or the Branch. Don't panic or run, just everyone lie down, it can't last. Look now where's your nearest Medical group, so you can call them if anyone gets hurt. That's about all the warning, remember the main thing is we're standing firm, no matter what happens we stand for freedom, we stand for..."

Barney stopped speaking, and immediately everyone heard the sirens, lots of them, and now, far away, the roar of engines. An audible sigh, a giant gasp, swept up from the crowd. Maggie had taken the microphone.

"Hullo this is Maggie here" she said. "I just want to say congratulations to all people, especially the women and children here, I think we have time for one more song, to keep our spirits up," Maggie started off, in a low clear voice, that boomed nevertheless.

Macker was up on the car, holding the radio mike close, to be heard above the singing.

"Yes we can see them clearly from here now" he was saying," armoured cars, coming over the bridge, um, I can see a watercannon and what looks like tanks or very large bulldozers, lorries three abreast it goes on and on. The last of the boats is just going out of our sight soldiers stuck all over it like dummies, as you say Brian that looks very like a diversion...And I've just been told there are helicopters coming in behind us! I'll pass you back to Brian at the barricade."

Barney was glancing through his notes, some moving words, some fine sounding phrases what more could he do? He felt Maggie's had in his gripped it and felt the returning squeeze. One of the young fellas tapped him on the arm.

"They look just about in range now" he said.

Barney took a deep breath and began. He had determined to start cheerful and friendly, something, he thought, like an early morning disc jockey.

"Sing away folks if you like" he began, "If you can hear yourselves above this thing. I'm told you lads in the army and police can hear me now. Well, good morning to you all from the North east CoOp, I hope you're not going to shoot me or anyone else here this fine morning. I have a list of items for you here, greetings, and some very long lists of relatives here in the street, and an appeal...Well lads the situation is this, we have eight or ten thousand people waiting on you'se here, maybe you can hear them singing. We're all unarmed and we're not going to move, no way. We're here as you know to defend the dock strike, the docks have been doing worse and worse these last years, and we want to get things going again. Only problem is there's some rich and powerful people losing out by it, and it's them, not us the people, who have the ear of the government. Each one of you lads has a choice to make this morning, are you listening to me? Will you obey the wishes of the corrupt and sold out government, or the wishes of the people, who in fact you were hired to serve and defend...!"

The front of the column was arriving. Old tanks, led incongruously by battered and paint splattered police and Special Branch vans. The branch pulled up to the left, by the river, and the riot police way over to the right. The three tanks lined up across the big wide intersection, and behind them the trucks started to unload.

"Well now friends" Barney persevered, "It's a choice you're going to have to make, we see you unloading your gas guns and your rubber bullet

guns, and you might as well know we're well prepared for them and we're not moving an inch. In any case there's no way for us to run. So you can decide for yourselves now, if none of you will fire they can't punish you all, you know that. But if you follow orders, its going to be the worst massacre ever. And you'll be murdering your own, the same people, strangely enough, that you were hired to defend. So that's the appeal now. It's a hard thing I know but you got to do it. Oh yes..."
Barney had waited till they started to line up in front of the tanks.

"I'm asked to say to you, the most important thing, if you'se get the chance to come over at all, just run across. We have breakfast waiting behind, and jobs and houses for you all if you want them. Now Maggie here has some requests and then we can get on to those lists of your relatives they want you to murder."

Anton Fowley was confused and afraid. Trooping out with the others from behind the water cannon and tanks. But more than that he was angry. He could feel the anger and excitement rising inside him. At some point he knew that anger would overcome his fear. But he was sure to be shot down. Should he try to run the fifty yards across to the crowd? Some woman was starting to read out names, he suspected his own brother and sisters might be there...Anton moved mechanically to the orders shouted by megaphone from behind. The soldiers were lining up, line after line, almost sheepishly to do their job. He felt himself shaking with fury, it was all wrong, but he couldn't bring himself to break rank...Then Anton Fowley did a simple, even childish thing. He lifted his arm and began to wave. Immediately his wave was answered. Dozens, then hundreds of people were waving, and the soldiers, yes they were starting to wave back! Maybe a few people recognised each other. But it was unlikely, in the weird arclights and strange clothing. There were shouts then, and laughter, and broad city voices cheering. And then everyone was waving and laughing on both sides. The tension was broken. The massive crowd was edging forward. A yard, five yards. At the front a big gang of women were pulling off their helmets and running forward. Throwing down their sticks and shields. Max was following through the gap.
Then she found herself suddenly flat on the tarmac.

At that same moment Barney's laugh could be heard, echoing up and down the street. In the next he saw flashes of light by the river. Felt himself flying. A shatter of noise, screams and crashing. Now clutching. Now struggling in a mass of shrieking falling bodies. Roaring himself in pain and terror.

Over by the river the Special Branch had opened fire. Shooting at the red
Cortina, which they rightly took to be a centre of communications. In those
horrific seconds the Free acted. Dozens of men ran forward from the still
assembled ranks of soldiers. A thin ragged line, some covering the soldiers.
Some firing back at the Branch vans. In those seconds too the dock defence
groups fired back, from up on the containers, though they never admitted it.
The plain clothes police were stopped dead. A petrol tank to one of the vans
exploded. Figures could be seen, burning and twisting, falling or plunging in
the river.

The same seconds. Barney was alive and awake, but pinned. The mike was
still in his right fist.
   "Hold your fire" he gasped into it, "You can stop firing now." People
were being pulled off him. He was up on his knees. Head ringing, seeing
double.
   "Stop shooting" he shouted, "Stop shooting you stupid stupid people."
But by then the Special Branch contingent were hiding, dying or dead. And
the dockers had ceased fire and the thin line of mutineers were blending back
into the lines. At the microphone Barney's ears were filled with screams and
sobbing.
   "Now everyone move forward slowly. You soldiers, if you're coming
over, come now. Otherwise, go back to your lorries. Repeat, all soldiers,
either come over now or return to your lorries."
Barney was up on his feet, staring ahead of him. People were getting up,
extricating themselves, and slowly moving forward. Silent and stunned by
the screams of the wounded around them. A few stray shots still rang out,
but were ignored.
   "That's it" Barney went on, "come on now everyone the party's over,
come on over to us now lads and forget about killing and murder...for fuck's
sake can we have first aid people over here now..."
Barney had looked down, stopped, suddenly couldn't go on, as he breathed
in waves of pain and nausea and grief, for the body below him was Maggie.
No, not Maggie anymore. Just a big lump of warm bubbling meat, with half
her face spewed across the tarmac. Barney felt himself falling, someone had
taken the microphone, others held him as he struggled feebly to embrace her
dead body. As Barney fainted he could hear wild cheering as the great
crowds merged and the confrontation came to an end.

Across where the army ranks had been, officers, like frantic shepherds
were trying to herd the men back into the trucks. But whole platoons, big

gangs, were disappearing into the welcoming crowds, and hundreds of others were darting through from further down the convoy, to be embraced by the cheering crowd, and quickly ushered back from the front. Then fist fights were breaking out and officers fired into the air, as the huge crowds moved right into the army convoy before the order was given to retreat..

"Clear a way, clear a way, clear a way."

Macker didn't know any more if he was a radio reporter or the announcer.

"For Christ's sake get the gate open wider! My friends are dying over here!"

Though the shooting had killed four and wounded dozens, it had only struck one small section at the from left of the crowd. Most people never even saw the dead and wounded. The Special Branch contingent suffered six dead, while the army column had only a few minor casualties, but had lost half of its force.

General Mulcahy and Commander Bruton arrived, without ceremony, for the meeting in Lerriman's back office, leaving a crowd of bodyguards and security men in the corridor outside. Lerriman watched coldly, his bulging eyes red from the sleepless night, as Mulcahy eased himself painfully into a chair at the plastic topped table. The immaculate Bruton shuffled in his briefcase, and smiled his ice cold smile.

"Okay Bruton, the security prospect at this moment."

"Right, the police and army and my own men are at present concentrating on Government buildings and vital installations. Reports are coming in that the General Strike is taking hold, but also many concerns are suffering attempted takeovers by their workers, which adds to the property occupied overnight. We can't put figures on it right now, and frankly we can't do much about it. Their media are calling for marches into the city at noon. These are bound to be very large, and uncontrollable in our present state. We are totally overstretched and..."

"Tell me one thing" Lerriman was rapping nervously on the table, "Why did you open fire this morning?"

"You yourself authorised us to fire as a last resort."

"Don't give me that! I have permission to fire warning shots if tear gas and rubber bullets failed...You've handed them a fucking huge propaganda victory...You'll have to discipline those men."

Bruton lifted the palms of his hands and almost laughed.

"So it's come to this..that we have to discipline dead men!"

"Well, no, damn and blast it! Are they all dead?"

"Six of them are. They only lost four..yet they win! Listen Sir, we fired to prevent a total mutiny. In hindsight we should have cancelled the whole Operation. We were played for suckers, their infiltration was worse than we thought, and of course they had complete details of our meeting yesterday...almost before we left that room!"

"Which brings us to the main business." Lerriman seemed somehow calmer as things got more desperate. "Have we no idea yet who talked?"
For once Burton stopped smiling.

"Not yet Sir, we're watching everyone in depth. It wasn't a bug. No breaks so far."

"Could it have been the Police Commissioner?"

"No no, and he didn't hear the details of our plans..to be straight, our first suspect is Peter Kennedy, General Mulcahy's aide."
Mulcahy spluttered with instant fury.

"That's rubbish Sir, Kennedy is completely loyal. His father was one of our best commanders."

"But some of his wife's family are in the Free."
Lerriman raised an eyebrow, jotted a note.

"Well find out fast for sure" he said. "We have to hit these people hard and soon and without any warnings. I want the leaders rounded up and interned. I want the Docks and all illegally held property taken back. I want plans along those lines right now!"
Mulcahy was looking down, but Bruton spoke up.

"Yes Sir. First of all we can't arrest the leaders, because basically they don't have any. That's their strong point. These people get their support by providing four things...food, housing, work and goods, in that order. The way to finally smash them is therefore to cut their supply routes, destroy their food and goods stocks and the factories, and only then, when support is waning, start taking back the actual property and making mass arrests. Otherwise we only provoke more opposition, as we did this morning, and risk more defeats and mass defections. Another priority is blacking out, banning, destroying and jamming their media."
Bruton paused, taking more papers from his case.

"I have a detailed operational plan here to finish the CoOps and the Free Unions, using our present forces, over a six month timescale. However, considering the level of infiltration, I can only guarantee this if I am given overall control."

"You want the Commissioner's job" Lerriman had been expecting this much. But Bruton was shaking his head.

"No I want to be commander of overall security. You appoint a new Commissioner of Police, you continue your Cabinet and the rest. But only the three of us here know the detailed plans. It's not democratic I know, but its a National Emergency."

Lerriman was thinking fast now, Mulcahy was a yesman, should he comply with Bruton's naked bid for power.

"Tell me" he asked, "What for instance does your plan say about today?" Bruton actually paused to take a sip of water before replying. He knew he had won.

"We announce to the emergency Cabinet and Security meeting this morning a new and detailed plan to attack the docks tonight, using a hand picked commando force. We let the spy report it, so they build up their defences around the Docks. then at an earlier time we attack and destroy their Supply Depots, all twenty two of them in the City, which will be lightly defended. We also destroy some of their transport, and then block off all routes out of the city to them, cutting their supply routes. I have all the operational and logistical information here. It's straightforward military tactics. They've murdered six policemen now Sir, and we plaster that fact all over our media, shock, horror, weeping kids..."

"That" Lerriman broke in "is the kind of thing I wanted to hear."

Peter Kennedy was worried and walking fast, head down, through the back streets to avoid the marchers and rioters who had virtually brought the city to a halt. Glancing back furtively at the Special Branch police, two on foot and three in a car, who followed his every movement. They were watching everyone of course, they had already turned over his house and found nothing. Before it had been easy, only now were the real dangers of spying coming home to him. Twice he had almost used the slim radio, which would be excuse and plenty for interrogations! Now his brain was whirling, as he crossed an intersection, weaving his way through a noisy workers' demonstration. He must give the message, yet he was not at all sure about his information. He cast his mind back again to the Cabinet meeting that morning. It had all been too pat, he had expected recriminations and histrionics, but Lerriman had come in late with Bruton and Mulcahy, and calmly announced the new attack plans. Not a word about the massive leak the day before, but lots of details about the new plan, at midnight, using commandos from helicopters and boats to seize the north entrance to the Docks and dismantle the barricade to let the main force through. And more plans for martial law, curfews and internment. Peter had tried to draw Mulcahy on the subject, ever so gently, but the old General for once revealed nothing. Yet he was hiding something..

"We'll out manoeuvre them this time!" he had said at one point, clapping his hands like a child. They knew, everyone knew there was a spy. Yet everyone was smiling at each other innocently, smiling their politicians smiles..It was a set up, he was almost sure, but he still had to send the message, what if he was wrong? Peter had decided to disappear into the Underground as soon as he could arrange it, he had done his best and the pressure was now unbearable. Still he walked, his mind racing round in circles...then he had a simple plan! He came to a phone box, and in a second he was in it, depositing his coin and rapidly dialling. And it was working! The Branchmen were approaching the door. The phone rang once..

"Hello Maeve?"

"Yes."

"They're going to attack by the North Road at midnight, securing the barricade with commandos from helicopters and boats, but its all a bit fishy."

His finger cut off the call, as one of the policemen opened the door.

"Sorry, then my mistake" he said as the receiver was grabbed from his hand. The cop put it to his ear, shoving Peter back, but the line was already dead. He pulled Peter out of the box, and the other caught him, shoving him back against the door..

"Okay who did you ring?"

"I...I was trying to ring my wife to say I won't be home."

"What's the number then" said the other, as two more heavies arrived.

"None of your business."

Peter felt his head crash against the door.

"Everything is our business, you're a spy man, admit it."

"What's the number then?" a fist dug him in the belly.

A small crowd was gathering.

"They're police. Leave him alone pig!" someone yelled, and the Branchmen were feeling for their guns.

"Okay its 279433" said Peter helpfully.

One of them fished for a coin, while the others pulled Peter away.

"But I didn't get through" Peter shouted back, "I told you it was a wrong number."

The Branchman paused.

"Either you're telling the truth or you're a smart bloody bastard...We'll walk together from now on, this following is ridiculous."

Peter didn't protest. It was pointless. In fact his heart was soaring with victory, as he made his way back to the Department of Defence, flanked now by six large policemen.

I got to get this down. Set it down now that Maggie is dead dead dead. Before this awful clarity of grief is rubbed out, like all the rest. Before it gets faded by time and by new griefs coming, like a heavy axe chopping rough soft bodies..Oh Maggie, even now the details grow fuzzy..but I can still picture clear your warm smiling freckled face. Oh Maggie you are gone forever..Can I even feel the same anymore, the mother, the sister, who would wrap up the whole lot of us in your overflowing love..Oh how pathetic I am, who cannot even hold on to her grief! That's why I really wanted to go with you at first, to let that fiery sorrow consume me. Set it down now! Can't I even hold onto my sorrow in the rush of events. Time is no healer, no, time is an anaesthetic, or a fucking obliterator!

But I can still see that minute clear, that long, long minute when the Special Branch opened fire. I see myself fighting and struggling through that tight gigantic mob. I see myself screaming out her name .. Maggie I knew you were hit, knew Barney was alive, even before his voice came back on the air. Before I ever arrived at that red car parked in a pool of blood. But I knew too late to save you Maggie, and it seemed like no one even cared. As I looked up from your body everyone was cheering and roaring as the army came over. As I helped Barney away from that place the first rays of sunshine came over the barricades. Poor Maggie, you died real quick, and another bleeding day had begun.

General Mulcahy climbed awkwardly out of his armour plated Mercedes, and almost ran up the stairs into the glittering hotel lobby. He was excited and confident. It had been a busy and fruitful day. Freed from the endless bureaucratic and politician charades which had become his life, he had issued a stream of clear and precise orders, following the details of Bruton's plans. The hand picked Commandos had been assembled and and a hundred logistical points attended to. Mulcahy was the centre of a military machine swinging into top gear, a sense of power and action had dispelled his doubts and fears. Even the old sickness in his stomach seemed eased, and as usual his lust for food had overcome his doctor's advice. It was Captain Peter Kennedy who followed him up the steps, with a posse of security men behind...He and Peter would eat well together, they deserved it.
Mulcahy took Peter by the arm, as they were ushered to a reserved area. He was very fond of Peter, his mannerisms, his calm youth, his brown skin, and at times like this when he felt good he had to hold himself back from taking his arm, or fondling his hair. He caught himself, sometimes, muttering endearments. Yet he had not revealed to Peter the details of Burton's plan ..that was the order, and he had grinned with delight at Peter's puzzled looks, when the military preparations obviously did not fit the proposed operation. A little surprise Peter would know soon enough. If he did not know they could hardly make more ridiculous accusations against him.

Peter followed Mulcahy to the table, across the deep piled carpet, and he nodded to the Branchmen, who took up another table across the lavish restaurant. Though he appeared his usual attentive, smiling self, in fact he was fighting down rising waves of fear and panic. He knew by now it was a set-up, they had never searched him, they had let him make that phone call. He must at all costs find out from Mulcahy what was going on. He feared above all that he would find out, and be too terrified to act.

Mulcahy was having a chat with the subservient staff, had ordered fresh salmon entrees for them both, followed by roast beef. Now the fat General sat back and glanced at his watch, he had a half hour to eat. Then he produced a case of slim cigars, Peter accepted one for later, desperately flashing his smiling blue eyes.

"This is a great treat Sir, thanks awfully."

"We deserve it my boy, we have done a great days work."

Peter leaned forward confidentially.

"To be quite frank Sir, I am rather worried. This business with the informer, what if they know our plans in advance again and, and, well to be quite honest sir, some of them don't quite fit in."

Mulcahy laughed, a deep throated gurgle, and stubbed his cigar as the salmon salad was set before him.

"My dear boy, of course you are worried, because you don't see the whole picture" he laughed again, as Peter's face remained puzzled and expectant. Now leaning forward himself, almost whispering, as Peter smiled into his stinking breath.

"We're not going to attack the docks" he said.

"We're not?" Peter rolled his eyes in feigned surprise. Mulcahy was shaking his head, shovelling in food already. He paused a moment.

"I think I can tell you now, we're going to destroy their supply depots, all those in the city, and their lorries and adjacent factories."Then he sat back, grinning, to watch Peter's response.

"G'Great" he managed to come out with. His brain whirling in horror. "A surprise attack at midnight, they'll all be down at the Docks I suppose."

"Exactly!" Mulcahy clapped his hands "Only not at midnight. We move at nine o clock!"

"Great idea Sir," said Peter. This was Burton's work and he knew it. "We'd better eat up so."

The General plunged back into his salad, and Peter ate a mouthful, while his head refused to think, and his heart leapt in sheer terror. Every minute now counted for lives. He must radio James. At any cost. But how? He ate another mouthful. Steeled himself,

"Excuse me Sir, I'll just slip out to the toilet."

Then he was walking to the door. And a Branchman was getting up. And following!

"Jesus Christ" he squeaked. Would he run for it? Could he hide? He glanced back again as he opened the door.

"Just taking a leak."

"Me too."

They were alone in the roomy perfumed toilets..."Got to get out, it's a trap! Oh fuck. Oh fuck" Peter was thinking. and then a sudden certainty.. "Got to get rid of this man."

He managed a few squirts on the pink tiled wall. Zipped his pants. The Branchman was still pissing.

"Great dinner in here" said the cop, as a surge of desperate anger rushed over Peter. He hit the man from behind. Whacking his face into the wall. And again, and again. As he collapsed the flush came on. Spraying yellow and bright red water down the drain.

Peter was on his knees. Frantic. Gasping. Pulling out the slim radio. And the aerial.

"James! James! Can you hear me James...oh Christ, oh fuck he's out of range...James! Oh come in for Christ's sake."

"I'm here. Don't panic. Using wrong name."

"Listen they move at nine, not the docks. The supply depots, all of them. Coming through the city" he gasped.

"Got it. Anything else. You all right?"

"No James. I'm in the jacks at the Grand. I just knocked out a Branch man. Maybe he's dead. I' I'm fucked James, there's loads more outside and the General eating"

"Listen don't panic. Hide your radio. Try a toilet tank. Say yer man slipped. Maybe you can get out."

"Yes yes I'll try it."

"I'll have some boys pass there in ten minutes or so."

"Yes, I'll try it, thanks James."

"Calm down man. Great work. Over and out."

Then Peter was rushing into the cubicle. Scrabbling with the cistern. Pushing the radio in. Falling. Getting up.

He stopped, took a deep breath. And opened the door. Across the dining hall the General was tucking in. But two more Branch men were coming towards towards him! He beckoned them forward.

"Hey your mate's hurt. He's after falling. Come quick."

The police glanced at each other. Then snub nosed pistols appeared in their hands.

"Don't be silly" said Peter desperately as they followed him in, "he's hurt bad, slipped and hit his head."

Outside Mulcahy paused, then went on eating, as Peter helped pull the man out of his piss and blood.

The man groaned deeply.

"Oh NO NO he's wakin up" Peter thought.

"I'll go and call a doctor" he said.

"No wait here you're under arrest."

But Peter was already out the door. Then he was running between the tables.

"Stop. Stop that man! Stop or I shoot."

A loud bang. Breaking glass, as Peter left the dining room. Belting down the corridor in total terror. Leaping into the wide stairway.

"Stop that man!"

Seeing the lobby below, men running. Tried to stop. More shots and falling in a black scream.

Then nothing at all. Peter Kennedy's body rolled to the bottom of the stairs. Tourists fleeing in panic.

Excited men closed in. Jerking their guns over the limp and broken body.

My name is Macker McDonagh, and to be honest I'm no writer yet. but I could be a storyteller. My father and my granda were that, and my Da was a poet too. We were travellers. Landless people from the west. No! I'm no writer, just a little gap toothed tinker, sitting here in this suite of offices, unarmed, guarding fourteen sleeping soldiers and whiling away the night hours with a pen.

Yes I could be a story teller but it's true. I am sitting here wide awake in the middle of a Revolution. After three days without sleep. And the whole of the State is falling apart, half the army has come over already and nothing can stop us now.

My father was a poet though he couldn't write, and a singer and a broken down actor in his youth. But he married Tina Kelly from the city. She was pregnant to be sure, so I was the reason that he done it, I was a trouble maker before I was even born. And for that he was cast out, by traveller and settled people alike. Them were the rules of life when I was born. We were out of the lowest of the travellers, black strangers hated by all. And the poorest of the poor though of us less than dirt. I am come from a savage and desperate people, beggars and alcoholics, survivors from the far past, crippled by close marriage and destroyed by the flood of modern life. My father is a dead man at last. Dead by his own hand in the mental prison where they put him. My mother is dead long since. I seen her die slowly, I seen my Da torturing her last days. And we joined in. That brutal innocence of children!

But I am alive all right, and I sit here writing by the yellow smoking lamp, waiting and waiting for the dawn, and watching my fourteen prisoners. One of them is snoring...

Below us the street is still busy though the lights are still off, lorries and carts and bikes and gangs of people going by. Shouts and running feet, this is no time for sleeping. It is true, I have come through clean, by a marvellous chance I have stepped out of the closing trap into some far future. I have lived here four year now, and rescued my brother and sisters and brought them here. And I have worked hard here, in this radio group and two days in the bakery, and in the pubs and theatres every week I do my show. Yes I am a scholar now! I can read and write and bear to live between four walls. My father never could do that..

But this is a free area, a different thing entirely. In fact the whole country will soon be a free area, after the amazing events of the last few days, we could be spreading all over the world! I believe now it could really happen, I am sitting here quiet in the centre of the great storm, the rich property owners, the cops, even the army are on the run. How else can this be? A giant drama is sweeping over us, yesterday at the Docks, when they shot down Maggie and Barney and the rest, I took hold of that bloody microphone and it was still working. And it was me speaking calmly to all the people and soldiers and police and out on the radios. Jesus Mary it was me squatting in the blood behind that car! I don't even know what I said, but I'm sure it was the right thing. Like as if I had been taken over by something else entirely, it didn't affect me. We won that fight, by trick and propaganda to be sure, but mostly by pure mad determination, and Maggie and Fergal and a lot more dead besides. But last night was something else. The Battle for the City! And a great victory no doubt, but it shocked me more than anything I have ever seen. To me and Max and anyone who saw those streets it was a nightmare you shiver and shake to think about! And you can't say I'm afraid of blood. My whole life has been a dirty bloody fight. I seen Maggie's brains spilt out that same morning, I been beaten half to death as a kid...but those screams! Half butchered half burned alive. Those terrible screams that only death can stop!

They are dead anyway and I'm alive to see the uprising rushing ahead. Two more army barracks have mutinied in the night, the city is ours, and today the takeovers really begin, the factories, the media, the government building, the prison gates flung open! I am a part of it, but when I stop I am really amazed, I'm more a passenger than a revolutionary, but Barney and them, they knew this could happen. They saw it coming ten year ago, a country without cops or rulers or rich parasites sucking on the poor. They wanted room and enough for everyone without private wealth and power, to work and live and learn and,even to be happy. The truth is that we made this happen ourselves! I would have been the first to say, even five year ago, that they were mad.

I am still here, the windows are a shade less black and the morning is coming. In two hours they'll be here for the prisoners. These ones will be let go to join the defence groups in their own areas. I'm writing better now, still forced but easier. Sometimes my head is full to bursting with ideas and stories, if I could just write them down. But what happened last night was something else, more incredible and wonderful and horrible than any play. I am going to write that all down...

I was standing up the front, with Maurice and Jenny and Dabser. It was our second Assembly in two days, called for one reason, to decide if we should use armed force to defend the Docks. We had been told in the morning that the army were planning another attack at midnight. All day thousands had been working, fortifying the whole area. Digging deep trenches and barricading all roads leading to the Docks. Work was still going on,but he Assembly was packed all the same. Work was still going on, but the Assembly was packed all the same. It was in the factory just back of here, a low wide building and much better than that barn in the Docks the day before. We had done our interviews and set up our equipment and, well, to tell you the truth it was routine. We were broadcasting parts of it all right, but without the big dramatic link ups we had in the Docks the night before. A lot of other places were having their own Assemblies that evening. There was this old codger going on in a pretty obvious speech about the dangers of confronting the State. Maurice had just got us tea and sambos from outside. Everything was normal. Then it all happened!

I actually saw her enter, a bicycle came full tilt through the main door, knocking one of the checkers aside, and belting straight up the centre aisle, dodging people, bell ringing..It was Max! First thing I thought was she must have cracked completely over Maggie getting killed, then I realised something terrible was up. I started to move, in and out towards her. But I only went a few feet when she was upon the stage. She grabbed the microphone and spoke, gasping for breath. She read a little note in her hand.

"We've just heard the army are coming to destroy our Supply Depots. All of them. They are coming through the city and will probably hit us first. They, they're starting at nine o clock that's...twenty minutes from now!"

She stopped. Suddenly clapped her hands over her face and stood there. I was getting on the stage by now. And a great murmur rising from the packed crowd, on their feet now, people barging through. Shouts, disbelief, the beginnings of panic. I was at her elbow, and Josie and Jenny, come to protect our friend. I wanted to call for a Defence Groups speaker. Then there was a roar and all heads turned. One, two, three, four motorbikes came right in the door. It was people from Defence HQ. The message had got through. A captain in the army lost his life getting that message through.

We pulled Max aside as the Defence Groups took over. The motion to take up arms was carried overwhelmingly on a show of hands, then they were running through an emergency plan. And a list sending different groups to different tasks. As they spoke the crowd went silent. Then people were calling out and running for the doors, as they realised there was something they could do. We could hear hooters, bells and sirens starting up, close by and far away, as the general alarm spread across the city. Then people were going a little crazy, jumping up and down, embracing under flags, darting back and forth in the aisles like trapped rats...

I remember running in a vast crowd. I'll never forget the sound of thousands of running feet. We started in the third big crowd, heading for the central shopping area. But I soon lost Max and Josie and Jerry. Glancing sideways I saw gangs of helmeted youths, surging down from the flats, flags flying. I was caught up in it, the whoops, the yells, the sheer power of the mob, as we turned a corner and swept down the hill into the city centre. Some street lights were still on. I glimpsed cars turning up and over, and policemen running away.

Then two lorries across the road, just beginning to burn. The crowd split and split again. I was with a smaller group, clambering over two barricades as they were being built. Into a smaller street and over another block, where a man was shouting instructions, and youths were methodically smashing the plate glass windows. I was near exhausted when I arrived at the last barricade. Just two cars turned up on their sides. Ahead of us an empty street, a few darting figures. I spotted Josie there already, in her red scarf, she was radioing urgently, and I thought I should be doing the same.
"Buses, lorries, anything you can get" I heard her say. Then her voice was drowned in the crash of plate glass.
"...be too late, less than five minutes. Over and out."
A hand on my shoulder. It was Max and Jerry. Then we were joining the work. Turning over cars. Dragging furniture out of the Department store on our left. Lots more people were arriving. I heard Josie on a megaphone..
"This is the last barricade in this street. Please don't go further. This is the last barricade in this street.."

A gang of us heaved together and another parked car went over. I glanced ahead and saw a grey van career into the empty street in front. For a moment I thought it would ram the barricade. But it screeched to a halt and two men flung open the doors.

"Petrol Bombs!"

In seconds a chain was formed. Passing the crates up and over the tangled wreckage.

"Everyone off the street. They're coming now." Josie was shouting.

"Everyone up on the roofs. This is your last warning. Take a crate with you that's the way. Everyone off the streets. They're coming in shooting!"

Me and Max were in the line, swinging the heavy crates. The street was still full and for the first time I was really afraid. Then I heard it. From down the deserted street. And the whole barricade hushed to listen. An eerie grumbling clanking noise. The roar of engines. Then we all saw it, a giant armoured bulldozer grinding round the corner just a hundred yards away. The next thing we saw was the muzzle of a tank!

"Off the street. Off the street. Off the street!"

For a moment I was too terrified to move. Then I was running, crate in hands, a crazy clambering run.

I remember that first RATATATAT burst of sub machine gun fire, as we blundered into the wrecked window display of the apartment store. Max was behind me, tripped and dropped her crate. Scrambled up and dragged the crate in behind her, bloody handed. Then we were following Jerry into the dark shadows. In and out of the counters, yells in the half dark.

"This way. This way. Everyone up stairs....."

As I reached the foot of the stairs there was this great rumble. Then a terrific, high shrieking and crashing. The bulldozer was going straight through our first barricade. I just got a glimpse of flying metal and exploding yellow petrol bombs. And the screech! No one on foot could have lived in that narrow street. I ran up two flights. Following the others through this music department to the front windows. I saw Jerry hurling tape decks through the glass. Then everyone was lighting molotovs, and flinging them out onto the army convoy passing below. The army tactics were brutal, but stupid enough, once they had lost the advantage of surprise. In a minute there were a dozen of us there.

"Take it easy. Take it easy" someone was shouting, "make every one count!"

I looked around and saw two men carrying in a third. His hair was all burnt off and his pants were sodden with blood. Suddenly I was mad. Throwing anything in sight out the broken windows.

A minute later Max was pulling my arm, to go and help guard the stairs, and

I followed her back with two young fellas. Downstairs was filling up with smoke, as fire licked through the Clothes Department. You could still see people down there. Black figures flitting and ducking. Hurling molotovs at the tyres of the passing armoured trucks. The other two fellas ran down to get them, as they went there were more heavy explosions further away. And in a minute the whole convoy was grinding to a halt. The head of it had met up with our armed Defence Groups. I seen it later, the bulldozer and a tank. Their treads blown off like useless toys and their guts burnt out.

"I think they've stopped."

"Everyone upstairs!" Max screamed.

When that convoy stopped the soldiers had a bad choice, to abandon their troop carriers or to fry alive. Suddenly there were soldiers inside the shop. Opening fire at random. One bloke got back up. Two were certainly killed. A fourth almost made it, but he was hit on the first flight of stairs, just below where we lay flat on our bellies. The bullet hit him in the back of the head and travelled up, tearing off his nose and one eye. He fell like a sack. His last eye is staring up at me still. For a moment me and Max lay paralysed with horror. Then we were retreating. She lit the bottles and I threw them down the stairs. Not stopping to see if our dead friend went on fire. It was mad. Bullets were whistling around us. But we had no other weapons and we had to block that stair. I whirled as an arm caught my shoulder. It was Josie, pulling me down.

"We're getting out by the roof. Can you hold on a minute just."

"What about the lift? Max shouted.

"Jerry wrecked it. I'll wait for you'se upstairs."

So we held on. But not for long, the smoke was suddenly too much. There were a dozen or so soldiers below. Firing up the stairs and at each other, then all rushing to the back of the store. I suppose they got out some way. The stairs was a sheet of flame, no need to guard it. But it was the smoke, black rubber and plastic smoke, that drove us, now coughing and half blind, up one flight after another, still lugging a half crate of mollies.

Suddenly it was much worse. We reached the top but we could hardly see at all, never mind find Josie. Max was pulling my wrist through one door. Then trying another.....I was panicking. Like drowning, I couldn't breathe, I was choking.

"Hold your breath" Max croaked. We were stumbling down a dark landing. Cleaner air. Then Josie, leaning out of a door, pulling us in and closing it.

I collapsed, racking and gasping for air, drenched in my own sweat. When I finally opened my eyes I was looking straight into those of a young soldier. My mouth dropped open.

"It's okay I'm with you" he said. I don't know how he got there. As we lay recovering in that carpeted office a masked search party came staggering in with two more stragglers. When they closed the door the smoke still billowed underneath. Like water in a sinking ship. Then we were being urged out the window, and up a metal ladder onto the flat roof.

"One at a time, but quick!"

The roof was crowded already and the sky was black with smoke. The air was crashing and shattering with explosions, bombs and artillery. We were in the centre of the battle for the city! I was still dazed from the smoke. Crouching a minute, then up and running to the edge, still clutching my half crate. Below I saw madness. Lorries burning and exploding, soldiers running. The first mad rush of our Defence groups had taken them half way down this column. Most of the troops had just thrown down their guns. They had no heart and no room to fight. But just back from us they had had time to group, behind the remains of our second barricade, firing machine guns up the street. Killing many of their own fleeing soldiers. Further back I could see lots of people, soldiers and Defence Groups alike. Crammed into doorways, hiding under and amongst the wreckage and burning. I followed Max and Josie onto the next roof. And there was Jerry with a gun, just picking off the soldiers at the barricade below. People were grabbing bottles from my crate. Then the soldiers were breaking and retreating, and scattering in terror as a whole shower of molotovs came down from another roof and began exploding amongst them. I seen an officer shoot a man in the back. I seen men on fire, rolling and screaming for mercy. Then we were all flat on our faces as an artillery shell hit the building opposite. Their artillery was totally senseless. When we got up I seen the soldiers fleeing in panic, some trying to surrender. And now our Defence groups were breaking cover too, charging and leaping down the street, whooping like Indians in their multicolours. Loads of them, appearing from everywhere. Waving and firing their guns, jumping debris and bodies, as they began their second charge, against the soldiers still resisting.

Then suddenly the battle had passed us by, and we were back in our own territory. It was like that everywhere, quick running fights, then surrender. The troops had no idea what they were supposed to be doing and most of them didn't want to fight at all. There was cheering on the roof tops. The late sun was setting below the blanket of black smoke. Blood red sun and black smoke. We were laughing and hugging each other, delighted to be still alive. Then all rolling on the tarmac roof as another shell landed nearby. As I write this an odd shell is still being fired from the hills. But by midnight we had captured all the key points in the sky.

A crowd had gathered round Josie and Max who were using the radio. People were trying to help the wounded, getting back into their groups or forming new ones. We had to secure the roofs, and half the street was on fire by now, and hundreds of civilians and soldiers trapped in the buildings. The fire brigades were right in the battle zone but they were overwhelmed, and later whole buildings had to be blown up to stop the fires spreading. For us it was work. Hot and dangerous and getting darker by the minute. I helped carry a stretcher down. This bloke had burns all over, moaning and crying at our every move. We got him down this fire escape to a rescued army lorry in the street behind. But he was dead by then and the lorry couldn't get out anyway. So back to the main street with our stretcher, and the full horror of it hit me..fire, glass, blood and new explosions. Mutilated and dying still laid out in the gutters, men, women, soldiers and corpses, some crushed or run over, some half roasted carcasses. It was like a vulture feast, with people dragging them back and dragging them back, as the heat rose and the fire..and smoke came down the street. I followed Digger, but I was dizzy and sick and crying all the way. We just rolled them roughly onto the stretcher, trotted round the corner, rolled them off, and back again. We must have done a dozen that way. From there they went again by stretcher, to the fleet of ambulances that couldn't get near. This was one of the worst places in the whole battle. Where the first crazy rush of our militias was stopped. And both sides opened with fire raining from above. My brain was filled with screams and urgent shouts. The army were holding a position at the main river bridge, but were about to be attacked from both sides. Newly armed groups were running through the carnage in both directions.

I will remember the faces, wet with sweat and excitement, and the faces of agony and the smashed faces of the dead. Doctors and nurses had come right in with stretchers. The fat mask face of a priest administering the rites. One by one the petrol tanks started exploding (they still used petrol) on the army trucks not already burnt out. Soon after we had to stop. I think some stretcher crews were killed. The Defence Groups just closed the road, let it burn, and worked to stop it spreading. They had check points already, and JCB's clearing way for fire brigade and ambulances.
We met up with Max and Josie again, and joined a big gang clearing buildings from the back...That was heavy dangerous work, but it brought me out of my shock. I think we were all glad to fall into it. I seen men with megaphones making up big groups of workers. There's a General Strike on, and thousands were still arriving from the North suburbs who had missed the battle. People have marvelled at it, my prisoners were saying it, but to us it came natural. I saw a school full of prisoners, and street kitchens staring up,

first aid stations, people queuing to give blood, lorries starting to get in and each building being checked over. In one shop they found six armed soldiers hiding in a toilet, and a dozen rioters hiding in the next room. It's horrible in some ways, how life goes on. Later in the night we saw houses already being occupied, and jams of Co-Op lorries moving out goods and supplies. There was plenty of personal looting. But one thing is cleared up, there's no more question of us laying down our arms. We have stolen the entire city, maybe the whole country, one day the whole world! The Revolution is happening and I seen it!

Well that's the story of the battle, or a bit of it as best I can write it. In the morning I have to see the radio group, they must all be exhausted like myself. We are taking over the top floor of a bank, or so I hear for our radio centre. There are lots of people occupying buildings and shops as well as the factories. I can see whole new areas appearing in the city centre..I am rambling, sleepy at last, this work has calmed me down. I will wake up Max now and try to sleep. Max was great today, with a thousand like her we could do anything...Jeezus I can still see that eye. That fella on the stairs with his one dead staring eye.

eight **max & macker**

It was the place of little hills and little lakes - thousands of them - stretching away across the border on both sides, and a maze of narrow lanes, winding up over the hills and down through high hedge tunnels. A place of little farms and fields, many overgrown with gorse and bracken and brambles. Nettles and reeds and little thorn trees facing East. To the west the hills rose, bigger and craggier, the farms more marginal, merging into the desolate mountains and bogs to the sea beyond.

It was a hard place, of hard people, and like all other places it had seen the trampling of foreign armies. The people driven out, the land divided, the survivors taken back as cheap labourers on the great new Estates. The new and littler farms broken out of the bad lands. The land and the people milked to the last drop. The land divided, till famine came, sweeping away whole clans and villages, where the best and the bravest were those who escaped after all.

To the north, where the hills levelled out, the foreigners had stayed and prospered, always afraid. And here, older survivors, a hard faced crew, who had seen the Land Wars, the slow grind of history and the decline of Empire.

Till the farmers were allowed to buy out their own land. War and more war, and insurrection, partition and Freedom! Freedom to vote for new politicians, to exist, narrow and mean, on a patch of land held fiercely, to watch the young people disappear to the cities. The old men remain, drawing the farmers dole, watching the land grow wilder every year, watching the guerrillas raiding north across the new border, and the armies of both sides trying hopelessly to seal it off. For a few decades things were looking up, a few advance factories, soon to be closed, better farm prices and tourists fishing the lakes, a few new settlers, hippies growing vegetables in the bad lands.

Bad times come round again, but not necessarily so. The tourists vanish and the farmers cannot sell crops or cattle. The old men remain on the shrinking dole. Poverty has struck in the cities and the economy of Europe is broken, cheap food is imported from saving countries.

Yet strangely enough the Co-Ops grew stronger, first with a string of tiny farms, then suddenly hundreds, crowds of city people. As if to break the stony soil by sheer weight of numbers. These people were organised, and they used their machinery, in fact everything they had in common. The old men were tempted soon enough by the camps, the life and laughter they had long forgotten, the storehouses where you could take what you needed, the new illegal pubs where the beer flowed freely. Still there was conflict, for in fact the Free were taking over, and they considered it their right to work disused land, to thin the trees, to rebuild the ruined cottages. Even to squat the newly closed factories and take over the lucrative smuggling rackets. The small farmers had no great choice, but to give them credit a few and then many of them threw in with the Co-ops. And some heartily, and with a dawning realisation...that another wheel had come full circle, for the clans of their ancestors had held this land in common. That they had survived, the guardians of the land, as if to renew some ancient culture. Or so the theory went, old fellas nodding over their pints. The Free had come, with their carts and tents, their buses and lorries and their children everywhere. A strange twist. In the little fields the reeds and weeds were once again giving way to the potato, potatoes to feed the city, potatoes and beet to fuel the lorries and earth movers. As the State become powerless and bankrupt, the Free did prosper.

Soon the final takeover had come, some said too soon, The great strikes, the takeover had come, some said too soon. The great strikes, the takeover of the ports, the sudden rise and fall of the fascists. Then the mutinies in the army, the defeat of the stalinists, the run on the banks...here in the country it meant just a few weeks of confusion, road blocks, armed renegades, and convoy of businessmen, clergy and a few big farmers fleeing north. Then it was all over and there was no law left, except the assemblies of the free Co-ops and Unions. But the world had finally taken note... a Revolution, and by example a threat to power, privilege and property worldwide. For even as the last popular takeovers were completed, the forces of reaction were gathering, like the storm clouds perpetually gathering in the western ocean. And everyone knew, some how, some way, that the insurrection must be destroyed.

Freewheeling, bicycles clattering, Max and Macker raced down the narrow twisting lane. Downhill between high hedges, dodging the bees and flies, and brambles that reached out to snatch at their faces. Faces sunburnt and radiant, flashing in the sun and shade, drinking in the warm rushing air that flung out their hair, then slowing, heaving and blowing, and finally to a stop. Then pushing their heavy laden bicycles up the next steep short hill. This was a holiday for them, coming down with all the kids to work on the farms, for this place was twinned with their own Co-Op area, and coming out as their turn cam up, on scouting patrols along the border.

"Beat yuh again" Max shouted, for she had pedalled a few yards further up the hill.

"My bike is heavier" Macker gasped, and with some justice. His bike included the tent and, strapped along the crossbar, an Armalite 180 carbine.

Max had left her bike, clambering up a little wall, after high sprays of huge luscious blackberries. Reaching up for the biggest and blackest and popping them in her mouth.

"Hey give us down a few of them!"

"Get your own"

Macker had laid down his bike, then steadied Max as she reached higher, almost falling back off the wall. He grinned his gap toothed grin, feeling the amazing silky curve of her brown legs, slipping his hands right up inside her shorts.

"Go on, gis a berry"

"Go away!" Max squealed

"Blackberries, blackberries."

Max twisted down laughing, to rub down a handful of them in his face, and fell off the old stone wall, almost knocking him over. They began kissing then, and licking off berry juices and sweat from each others faces.

The two of them were just getting into it when there was a loud RAT TAT TAT and a tractor and thresher appeared over the hill. Its sound, baffled in the hills and hedges, now bouncing wildly down the boreen. It was driven by an old man with a huge toothy grin on him, he pulled up, barely missing the cycles. Switched off. Max and Macker pulled apart as a high lilting voice cut the silence.

"Hulloo"

"Howaya" said Max. "We're the scouts up here for tonight."

"Sure if they came down here they'd drive in the ditch gawking."

"Did you see anything" said Macker, changing the subject.

"Not at all, but ye heerd I suppose they came over the morning down the border?"

"Yeah we did that."

There was a wee man killed, as far as I hear. But sure there's no use watching this road, there's plenty will phone across if they see anything sure."

"We'll be watching the back road as well" said Max rubbing her face.

"Aye well rightly that's the wild lonely road. I'll tell you what will do now childer see that ridge, above with the broken tree. There's a spot there and a wee field where they camp, you can see both roads and hear a motor five mile away."

Max nodded, barely catching his speech.

"That's where we're headed all right." said Macker.

"Good so" the man was a talker. "Ye have your radio now? There is a wee path up through the gorse, ye's can't miss it. Put up your tent there, and the night will come down over ye, gazing down over the sweet countryside below." The old man had clambered down off the tractor, still grinning like an old goat through his whiskers, and now spoke into Macker's ear, "And you can love each other to your heart's content, and nary an old farmer to bother you."

We'll be off then sir" said Macker, but the old man had him by the arm.

"You're lucky wee man" he said "I'll be kissing your bride and I'll be away off with meself."

As the man spoke he took Max by the shoulders, kissed her and went grinning and limping back to his tractor.

"Put up your tent mind, there'll be a storm the night" and the tractor bellowed.

"Bleedin bride" Max laughed "I'll be no one's bleedin bride!"

Max and Macker pushed their bikes around the corner and on up the hill. The sun had dropped, but it was hot enough still and dusty. And the high weeds dying of thirst at the tarmac edges. Then down a little hill, whopping, and nearly to the top of the next, where they unloaded, and chained up the bicycles in the thick bushes. The place was right on the border, and it was silent and deserted. Silent, only for a lark, fluttering high above them. Then even the lark was silent. It was so quiet that Max found herself whispering, as they exchanged swigs from the water bottle, before setting out. Just a few miles south the countryside was buzzing, with harvest in full swing and thousands down out of the city to help. And all the Defence Groups and ex-army units busy co-ordinating themselves, digging trenches and bunkers, setting up machine gun nests and artillery positions, mining road and bridges. For the Assemblies had voted to resist any invasion in depth, all the way.

To Max it still seemed unreal, as she shouldered her heavy pack and followed Macker through the furze bushes. How could you visualise jet planes in these peaceful hills, or tanks roaring up these narrow lanes? Yet just a minute later they had their first sighting of the enemy. A faint clatter, and Macker was pointing to a fat black dot, hovering far to the north. A helicopter on patrol, probably sniffing for mines or arms dumps. Max took the radio from his pack and reported in. Something to report! Then Macker swung the gun across his skinny shoulders and led the way on up. It was a hard climb, and prickly, and soon they lost the old sheep path completely. Through thickets and boggy places and up a little gorge full of trees. Then up and up, and a kestrel, fluttering above them in the unreal blue of the sky. Hovering higher, and always a little higher, to mock their grunting sweaty climb.

Macker was pressing on ahead, leaving Max climbing steadily. He loved this place, glancing always up and around him like a wild thing. Calling up at the hawk, then turning back to show Max the way up the steep ledges. For Max was in no hurry now, just climbing, and letting Macker go ahead. She felt sharp pains stabbing under her ribs, and hoped they wouldn't get worse. Just climbing, and always, far far off or suddenly louder, she heard a helicopter, gnawing like a pain, like the sudden fear growing inside her. Something terrible would happen! She was afraid, for herself, for Tommy, for Barney. And for Macker this skinny, sick, gap-toothed tinker she had taken in, oh, it must be five years back. She had been his friend first, and only recently had they become lovers. But now she loved him, his strong wiry body, his toothy smile, his flashing wit and genius, his outrageous vaulting ego. They had come down with the kids, Tommy, and Macker's young sisters, Kathy and Tricia. They were an odd but lovely family, Max thought, coming down together in the convoy of Co-op lorries. But what if..

"Come on lazybones, this way through the cottage."
Macker appeared, waving his arms against the sky, and vanished again. Macker the actor, the clown... Sure enough here was a cottage, three of them in fact, and a famine wall, almost flattened. Houses filled with nettles, the people swept away completely. Thistles, the hawk crying loud and wheeling

right away. And the helicopter suddenly loud and louder again. Max stopped a moment, breathing heavily, and in a moment everything became brutally clear. When she climbed on over the broken wall she noticed her face was wet, but she no longer afraid. for she felt, she knew for sure, as if she had seen the broken bodies in the rocks, that everything was lost, including young Macker McDonagh for sure. The fat bug helicopter faded and faded and was gone, and Max reached the flat rock, and there was the broken tree. And indeed a tiny meadow of high green grass, buttercups and dandelions and cow parsley gone to seed. And Macker singing as he pitched the tent already.

It was late evening but still light, Max and Macker lay side by side on the ridge, gazing down. Nothing moved, as if the wind itself were holding its breath.

From there you could see the two lanes close, in fact you could see a third. But more you could see, it seemed, the whole of the north, away north to the mountains, away east across a maze of silver lakes, to another faint blue line of hills. And to the west, ridges and higher ridges, and a glimpse of big mountains, heavy clouds and shafts of late sun. And below them, a million little fields and hedges run wild, hills and valleys and steeples far away.

It was dead calm now, and hot, but Macker was up and running for water, and back, getting up and flopping down, chattering about his media group, delivering one line gags. While Max fell silent, her eyes were focussing on nothing, and pushing him off roughly when he tickled her.

"Tell you what Barney, Macker I mean, you start the fire and I'll watch the roads, I'm knackered."

Macker looked in her eyes, crouching over her, then raised his eyebrows and smiled.

"Okay I'll do that, I don't mind" - and he set off happy enough it seemed, to gather some wood.

"Is he so shallow then" she thought and "that he doesn't even mind being called Barney by me?" But she pushed the though away, no, Macker was never shallow, for he could feel his way in with people and see through their eyes, that's how he could invent so well, no he was just young and excited, and elated with sex and freedom.

"I'm not so old myself" she said out loud, feeling the last sun come hot on her sunburnt cheeks. Max sank down into the mossy bank and breathed deep, feeling a great weight of exhaustion and sadness pressing her down. Her tiredness, her guilt, her tension, eight years, had she ever stopped! The work and the rush and the excitement, they had all been carried along with the movement, and she had been a seemingly endless source of energy and optimism. The squatting and the first Co-op, then splitting the Co-op in two as it grew itself, always new people, new faces to be fitted in. Then the Free Unions starting up and the mass strikes and takeovers beginning, and the Revolution itself and that had only been the beginning. Endless meetings and assemblies.. work that was supposed to be equally shared, with everyone enjoying wealth and leisure and new opportunities. But for the old hands it had been work, endless mounting work. Max had pushed herself round the clock, harder and further, immersed in the struggle and ignoring her own problems.. Barney of course, and Tommy, she had not been a good mother, she thought, she had been crazy to stay in that house, with Barney's eyes always on her. She had stayed for Tommy's sake, she couldn't always dump him in the nurseries. Not that she hated Barney, she would go back with him even now, and for a few weeks it would be fine. Then the old tension, the patronising, the guilt, the anger not expressed and building up inside her. And so many things and no time. And the terrible sickness that attacked her in the night. She would leave that house. It would be better for all of them. Max pushed those thoughts away, and immediately she was worrying about the Co-op, the shortages, rationing, the blockades and the impending invasion. No matter that their ideas had caught on and worked, virtually abolishing inequality, privilege, sexism and wage slavery. All the more reason to destroy them, wherever they sprung up, before they undermined the system of profit and power worldwide. Her thoughts whirled in familiar circles, but gradually she pushed them away, breathing deeply and pressing into the earth. Now staring at, but not really seeing, a distant plume of smoke, rising from a gorse fire on a distant hill. Hearing, but no longer noticing the birds, and a dog barking very far away. As slowly her mind emptied of distractions, her eyes unfocussed and her nagging doubts faded away. Max was not asleep, far from it, but if Macker shouted and sang at his camp building, she heard nothing, for she was floating, drifting, slipping and then falling gratefully into the timelessness of trance.

Time passed nevertheless, a few minutes which could have been years, and Max was blinking herself aware. Tracing the laneways below for possible movement. Seeing and smelling and hearing, and wondering anew at the beauty of the country below, held so firmly in such a murderous and divided history. She heard the lowing of milch cows. Below her the birds and the campfire crackling behind, and Macker singing, oddly..

"Oh me darlin. Oh me darlin. Oh me daaarlin Clementine." Max rolled over to see him.

"Jayzus Christ Macker" she called "Are you near ready I'm only starving!"

It was a hot night, but still rain did not come. Though lightning shimmered in the distance, the thunder came down from the west, long and rumbling. Rolling down out of the mountains and echoing in and out of the glens. Max and Macker lay naked in the meadow grass, overlooking the dark countryside. Macker was dozing off now, exhausted, while Max fiddled with the transistor dial of the radio, burst of music, and static, local Co-Op stations, the same news of the border raid that day,...then a foreign voice spewing propaganda...the takeover by foreign backed terrorists, the atrocities against foreign citizens and companies, the dangerous vacuum of authority, the need for swift action to restore the democratically elected government..Max switched to short wave, but Co-op frequencies were still jammed, she switched off cursing under her breath.

"Wake up Macker you lazy whore."

"And how could I be a whore?"

"They do exist you know, male whores."

"They do? Now there's a job I'd fancy. A whore!" Macker rolled over in the grass.

"Ah no Macker, sure you wouldn't be able for it."

"Oh wouldn't I!"

"Tell me something. Were you mad at me calling you Barney today?"

"Heartbroken."

"No seriously" Max was leaning over him, shredding a reed with her teeth.

"Course I wasn't mad. Barney's my friend, you're my friend..sure I know there will always be something between you but..Oh I dunno." Max was stroking him now, but he didn't respond.

"But anyhow" he went on, "if you can't tell the difference between us that's your problem."

"Don't be silly, it was just a slip of the tongue."

There was a long silence, but for a dog barking miles away. Then another distant rumble of thunder. Eventually Max spoke.

"I think we should send the kids home tomorrow Macker, I think this invasion could happen very soon, what do you think Macker really?" there was a shorter silence.

"I just don't know...the media groups expected it months ago. The naval blockade isn't working yet, we're too self sufficient, and we're gaining support all over, despite the news blackouts. Even this week there have been demos and bombings all over Europe at least, none of it reported except by our radios which are nearly always jammed out..Lots of people know what's happening, or they guess, but..I don't know Max cos it's all like military governments, there's nothing at all solid to stop them just wiping us out..I mean, we did have some luck, the peace missions, and all the fuss we made about disbanding the army, that was all good propaganda but it's too late for that now."

"What if there were uprisings in other countries, I mean, they were getting pretty strong."

I don't know Max, nobody does, sure it could be happening now and we'd hear fuck all about it."

The thunder rolled again, and a little breeze sprang up. Max sat up, and shivered.

"Let's get dressed I'm.."

"Shhh."

They heard engines. They were up, scampering to the edge, Macker cursing as he stood on a thistle, and they watched as two pairs of dimmed headlights travelled slowly up the twisty glen.

"Our lorries" said Macker "I know the sound."

"Smuggling. Better report in anyway I suppose."

As she spoke a sudden gust of wind rustled the bushes, they moved closer and embraced.

"You know something" she said "I haven't felt so good for ages."

"You're mad for the profound remarks, anyway."

"Funny ha ha you old...."

There was a loud crack of thunder, followed by a rumbling, from the north, long and low and trembling.

"Let's get the fire going again" said Macker.

Max felt a cold splash on her cheek, as suddenly the whole landscape lit up in a blue white lingering flash.

"Rain!" Macker was running towards the tent, while Max whooped like a red indian dancer, snatching up their clothes and whirling around.

"I'm the witch of the mountain!"

"Hey Max give us me trousers."

But Max was laughing madly, round and round, yelling and leaping, as if to catch the next shard of lightning that snaked across the sky. As the thunder clapped and wind rushed up over the ridge. Macker saw her throw back her head and laugh, as the first rush of rain splashed off her, and he was running for the clothes, retreating to the tent, as the storm broke violently at last above them.

"Come you crazy woman!" he yelled, as the tent pegs flew and lightning split the sky. But Max preferred to dance, writhing with the broken tree and rolling with the thunder, arching and spinning, crying out louder and falling, thrashing and struggling up, and screaming into the wind as it threatened to whip her away. Then off into an even more manic rhythm, splashing and twisting and crying and finally collapsing into the muddy reeds.

Macker sat cross legged at the open mouth of the tent, singing softly, shaking his head clear as wave after wave of sleep assailed him. It was almost three o'clock, he would wake Max at four. It was cold now, and high above the clouds were breaking up after the storm. He pulled his damp coat around him, and once again his hand went to the radio. He had been listening off and on to the Free Radios, to news bulletins and discussions that became more worrying by the hour. Something big was happening. A string of politicians had last evening been giving almost hysterical speeches...The Black Menace, the Trojan horse in the camp, imaginary atrocities being gloated over, exiled Ministers calling for an uprising against the Free, a new tightening of the blockade. The Free were still insisting on an unaligned position and protesting strongly, but it seemed to Macker to be hopeless, how could they compete with such propaganda? For truth had long ago become irrelevant, as a mounting fever of fear and mass destruction gripped the world, and country after country was plunged into bloody war, permanent and spreading around the globe.

And in a little tent on a little hill on the border, sat one more young soldier, rifle across his knees, trying to stay awake, trying to make some sense of a power mad and perverse world. For they had wanted to do away with centralised power, and all the forms of authority, which had led the world to this continuous war which now threatened to engulf them. It was cold, suddenly, and Macker was still peering into the dark bushes, seeing shadows move, and fearful now for his own life, and for the woman who groaned and muttered in her sleep behind him. He re-tuned the radio, and new and more frightening news! At an all night meeting delegates from the Co-Ops and Unions had elected a Temporary War Council to co-ordinate all the defence forces. Something was badly wrong, for the delegates had no agreed power to set up such a centralised Council. Macker couldn't believe it, he had covered many of the Assemblies, and knew full well such a proposal would never be agreed. His amazement deepened when he heard on the list of the War Council, the name of Barney Maguire. He clambered out of the tent, gazing up, puzzled, as the moon edged out of the scudding clouds which still gathered around the western mountains.

Straining his eyes, Macker walked round the edge of the hollow, then stood gazing down as the moonlight spread over the still countryside. Something had woken the lapwing, and their lonely beautiful whistles drifted from the fields below. He heard his own voice.

"The wind has bundled up the clouds,

High over Knocknaray
And thrown the thunder on the stones,
For all that Maeve can say."
He couldn't remember the next line, standing there, then his heart leapt! Something was rustling in the bushes!... away down to his left..Macker swung down his rifle and dropped into the reeds, for he had been foolishly silhouetted against the sky..A sheep or fox or badger surely..or an enemy unit scouting, the hired killers coming to get them! He lay there for ten minutes or so, his pounding heart subsiding as stillness prevailed. For if there was a man down there he could move neither forward or back without Macker hearing him. Then there was a low beep beep beep ... behind him. The radio! Macker was bounding to the tent, dived in, and found the switch.

"Patrol sixty three okay" he said.

But instead of words he heard a jumble of letters and numbers. He was groping for the pencil and pad, which were clipped onto the radio case... They were using code, despite the scrambler.

"Repeat" he said, and the message came again.

"Okay thanks, over and out" he switched off. Max was stirring, turning and moaning in her sleep but she did not wake. Macker found the torch and looked for the code key, as scores of others were doing, in little tents all along the border. He sat with torch and pencil at the tent mouth and worked it out..

"BIG RAID DOWN THE EAST GOT THEM WATCH CLOSE USE CODE."

Eleven words. Macker read them over and over, coming back to the two words "GOT THEM." He could readily imagine the scene ... armoured columns trundling down winding roads like these ones in the dark, thundery night ... Driving through unstopped to murder and destroy.. Then finding their retreat cut off, roads blocked, bridges blown, and guerillas closing in around them from all sides..." WATCH CLOSE"... yes, a diversionary attack was likely, but hardly this far west. Another thought struck him, there was no need to tell the scouts about the raid, they'd know soon enough, four words would have done -"WATCH CLOSE USE CODE" -.. No, the Defence Groups were giving them credit. They must have done well, reporting the column of course, maybe taking a lead in cutting the retreat.

Macker shivered, imagining the soldiers crouched in their armoured cars, just thirty miles away, awaiting a terrible death..But the Free would take prisoners, if they surrendered, prisoners to hostage, of course! His head was spinning, he thought of waking Max, and crept up beside her, feeling her warm breath and smelling her mudstained body. No, he thought, let her sleep awhile. Let her keep watch in the shadow worlds. He himself was wide awake now. Then he scampered back to his position on the ridge..

Macker lay there, shivering in the grass, for a long time. He tuned in, very low, for the four o'clock news, but the raid was not reported. He was surprised, then angry. Was this then the first action of the Temporary War Council, to censor the news? He turned to a foreign station, but their news as nothing but war hysteria. He switched off, shaking with anger. Then he was whirling around to the sound of a muffled explosion, from far to the east, and another, no that couldn't be thunder. And then from behind him, came a long terrified shriek!

Macker almost leapt off his feet, released the safety catch and almost shot Max as she blundered out of the tent. They ran together and embraced, Max was sobbing.

"Christ Max, I nearly shot you, what the fuck happened?"
For a minutes she couldn't reply.

"Oh M'Macker I had a terrible dream, I thought it was real, it was, it was.."

"It's okay Max you.."

"You were dead Macker, I seen you dead an little Tommy dead an Barney an Maggie and Frances and the kids.."

"Fucking hell" Macker broke in "what was it a nuclear bomb?"

"It was them" Max was pointing east "them bastards they're fucking animals they.."
Even as Max spoke there came another explosion louder from the direction she was pointing. Max fell to her knees.

"Wh' What was that?"

"Well now" he began reluctantly "there's a big raid, but away to the east and we have them trapped, I uh, I didn't wake you cos you were so tired."

"It's happening Macker. It's happening" she gasped.

"No listen" he squatted and gripped her shoulders. "Listen to me now, your dreams aren't always right Max, it's just suggestion that's all like, we're here to guard the border, you're afraid of what'll happen .. hey presto you dream we're all dead, that's it Max, you know that. Sure they'd never get us all anyhow."

"You're sure" she didn't believe him for a moment.

"Course I'm sure, it must be all in you head, sure we had a wild night of it."
Max's shaking had subsided to a shiver. Of course they must die, but she'd fight it all the way. Macker was only hiding his own terror.

"Right lets make some tea now and get you dressed warm. You're going to have to watch, I'm falling asleep."

Macker broke out the little stash of dry wood, cleared the sodden ashes and started a little fire. By the time Max had dressed and tried to wash he had made the tea.

"Here you are then, are you recovered. So?"

"I'm only freezing that's all" she said, hopping about in front of the tiny flames.

Macker got up, to give her a hug, but at that moment the radio bleeped.

"Yes, patrol sixty three come in."

"There's a big force to the north of you, can you see anything?" the rapid voice was not in code.

"Nothing, wait, a light moving about five mile north" said Macker.

"I hear engines" Max called from the ridge.

"Hello, we can hear engines .. oh fuck, helicopters!"

They had both seen them, in the faint eastern sky, a line of black dots, buzzing..

"Hello base we have about er, eight helicopters, coming from the East, straight for us!"

"Hello sixty three, get under cover and open your emergency instructions. Radio silence. Good luck. Over and out."

Max was scattering the little fire, stamping the embers into the mud. Macker was ripping down the tent and hurling it into the bushes. In half a minute they were deep in the thick gorse below the ridge. But the helicopters were almost overhead already. Gunships and great clattering troop carriers whirling in, searchlights probing the hill. Then a burst of gunfire. Max had her knife out and slit the lining of her jacket to retrieve a sealed message. Macker was trying to see what was happening, several helicopters seemed to be landing, on either side of the west road, others were turning south, he longed to use the radio. Then both of them were lying flat in the thrashing gorse, as a huge troop carrier came in right over them, preparing to land right where their campsite had been! Macker hid his head, too scared to move, but he heard Max's hoarse voice above the racket. Next thing they were crouching together, reading the emergency instructions under a glimmer of torchlight.

"Head For The Only Large Tree, 250 ys NW of Broken Tree Hill. 30 yds West of Tree is Overgrown Hillock. At Centre is Bunker Under Branches. Switch On Set. Turn Wheel To Zero. Wait 15 Secs. Press Red Button. Memorise And Destroy this NOW."

Max leaned over and kissed Macker on the cheek. Then she tore up the note and shoved the pieces in the mud.

"Let's go then love" she said, and he followed her.

Crawling , running, climbing. Fending off brambles that ripped at their clothes and skin. Max and Macker came quickly to the edge of the bushes. They stopped there, peering into the first dawn. Just three small fields separated them from the little overgrown hill. But a second helicopter had landed further down, and they could just make out figures leaping out and dispersing. It was rapidly getting light.

"Crawl behind the walls, come on" said Max.

Macker pulled the rifle strap tight and was following her along a tiny ditch, now through nettles and brambles, now through mud up to their thighs. His heart was pounding, he was terrified, he had never crawled so fast in his life. At the corner of the first field he caught up. Max was lifting down stones from the little wall, to go through without standing.

Then they were both face down in the mud .. Voices in the next field, then trampling feet!

"Fuck this for a bloody picnic."

"Hurry up Harry."

"Silence there. You men set up your guns behind this wall."

For a minute they lay there trapped, listened to the heavy engines, throbbing louder and louder, up the twisty glen.

"Hey men. Bring those guns down to the next wall."

"I wish he'd make up his bloody mind."

"Come on then, heave ho!"

The moment they were past Max was pulling down more stones. Oddly she felt dead calm now. Just like a game of den she thought, only if they were caught they were dead. Then they were crawling again. Half way across the last field Max stopped.

"Holy shit" she said. A group of men were coming back up the field towards them. "Pretend we're with them. Follow me."

Max stood up boldly and clambered over the wall. Macker followed her along the other side. Laughing and cursing the soldiers came by and over the wall just behind them. They were nearly at the thickets. Macker glanced back. Three shadows were following them!

His mind flashed, and he spoke..

"Up the hill mateys" he said pointing after the rest "You're not with us."

"Oh, right sorry mate" the soldiers turned away.

They reached the undergrowth and were crawling frantically through thick branches and thorns. Macker got through first, and was scrabbling with a pile of branches at the centre. Max flashed the torch once, and was tugging at a piece of rope. The hatch swung back and she jumped straight into the black hole.

"Max, Max" said Macker, but his words were lost in the roar of engines. Then the torch flashed in the hole. Max found the control. Unwrapped it, pulled up the aerial and switched on, turning the dial to zero.

"One thousand and one one thousand and two one thousand and three." Macker raised his head cautiously among the bushes, in time to see the outline of the first tank crossing the bridge on the road just below.

"One thousand eleven one thousand twelve one thousand thirteen" Macker ducked down, put his arms over his head.

"Jeezus forgive me" said Max, and pressed the red button. Then the whole world was shaking apart in one gigantic explosion on both sides of them. Macker slithered head first into the hole, as debris came crashing through the undergrowth.

"Get off you fucking eegit" he had landed on top of Max. He clambered up again, hoping to inspect the damage. Max's head appeared and she began pulling over branches. Closing her ears to a desperate scream, which kept coming over and over again.

"Get in Macker they'll see you" and Macker obeyed, as a machine gun opened up nearby, and others joined in, men firing in blind panic at the shadows around them. They pulled branches over and let the trap door drop. They crouched side by side on the muddy floor of the hole. And Macker composed a message .. "63, SUCCESS, DEAD AND INJURED" which Max translated laboriously into the code of the day. In reply they got two words .."GOOD, SILENCE." She switched the set off, and they tried to make themselves comfortable. Pulling rocks out of the walls to avoid sitting in water. Above them the firing had ceased, but they heard more screams, and shots and running feet nearby. And soon there were more explosions.

nine refugees

It was Peter Duggan spotted them first, mainly because he was the first to reach the top of the high ridge. They were about two miles below, down on the little mountain road, which ran up the long winding valley.

Peter managed a curse, as he fell forward into the wind blown reeds and heather on the ridge, he was gasping for breath, laying there watching the small antlike figures, which appeared one by one from behind a rocky crag, and toiled incredibly slowly up the steep hill. Then a knot of people round a hand cart. Tinier figures, children and a pram. Refugees!

"Fucking shit." He closed his eyes, trying to bury himself out of the bitter wind that whipped up over the ridge. He was exhausted, his head ringing from that last steep climb. For the last hour he had kept himself going by thinking of the hot soup they would cook up, in the little cave above in the rocks. But now they would have to go down, right down into the valley. Max would insist on it. And for what? To dash the hopes of his straggling band. These lost fools, wandering in a free fire zone on a mined road. And they would be sending them back to their deaths, the last enclave was full, there was no food, no space left, every house every village every barn was packed with destitute refugees who had ended up on this side of the army offensives. Very soon there would be famine.

Peter heaved himself back onto his knees and glanced back. Max had been following him up the steep track, she was almost up with him now. And Billy below, zig zagging up the steep slope. He looked again down over the ridge, slanting his eyes into the cold wind. He counted about twenty five of them, moving painfully slowly if at all, he could make out a bigger one waving his arms furiously at the front, and he could easily imagine the long journey which had brought them here. He had seen many, heard their stories, but these were totally desperate surely, to be climbing up through this no mans land in the short winter's day. City people, probably, who had fled the bombing and the shelling, the massacres of two months before, when all roads west were jammed, meeting always fresh destruction, and somehow eluding the invaders, who rushed in great mechanised sweeps, then stopped to consolidate their gains, killing and burning. Then moving again, leaving prison camps and work camps behind them. The new native army and police, all the gombeen men and informers, who sprang up like magic in their wake. But these refugees were still ahead of the army, just about, still fleeing the camps and the shattered towns for the endless roads, struggling with sickness, cold and starvation as well. Somehow eluding the sudden, meaningless massacres from the air, and finally reaching the borders of the last free area. Only to be turned back again! There seemed always to be refugees, wandering round forever, endless roads...

Max swung her pack down and dropped by Peter, panting.

"There's refugees below" he said, reluctantly.

"Where..Oh yes" Max was staring into the wind, then unpacking the field glasses. Could it be a trap?

Peter felt, rather than saw a subtle change in the light. He looked south, high, thicker clouds were dimming the brightness where the sunlight had reflected through. Below, on both sides, the land was suddenly darker. And there! Coming up the valley towards the, a roll of white topped cloud.

Max kept on peering down at the little antlike column, until the low cloud blanked out the scene. Crashing silently into the rocky walls below them, and billowing up, like a gigantic ghostly wave. Rushing silently up over the heads and curling down behind them.

Specks of white whipped past them in the mist.

"Fucking snow!" Peter shouted. The first snow of winter. Max's shrug was unnoticeable under her bulky clothes.

"Listen." She yelled in his ear, "We'll cut down to the Black Bank. Eat there and wait on the refugees."

Peter nodded enthusiastically.

"I'll go on and cook, you tell the others," she shouted, slapping his shoulder, and before he could reply she was a black shape, fast fading into the swirling mist.
Peter turned his back to the wind, pulled off his outer gloves, and blew on his numb fingers. Then he fumbled for the radio in its plastic wrapping, and consulted the code of the day. At that moment Billy appeared.

"Come in all, come in all," said Peter, then waiting for them to find and turn up their radios. "We have sheep below. Meet at number one four four. Hitler is cooking."
Billy had fallen flat and exhausted as Peter listened to the replies.

"Bogtrotters One four four. Nice one."

"Skyhawks. Adjust the flight plan."

"Fucking snow here" said Michael.

That was all. They were four groups, thirteen people, travelling parallel across the mountain wastes. Peter chuckled, pulling on his outer gloves, the enemy would make nothing of that, even if they picked it up, faint voices talking riddles in the mountains. And he was pleased, for once, with Max, their bitter and relentless leader. Usually he resented her fanatic energy and her personal attacks, they were not even supposed to have a leader. But she was the one who took over, driving on the demoralised guerilla. Everywhere the Free had fallen apart, when it became clear that the war was lost. The activists were reduced to fighting a guerrilla war, and merely supervising the retreat and organising rationing. Max's group was reduced to a bare dozen, lightly armed, assisting in the hopeless task of defending what was little more than a big refugee camp in the western wilderness. Peter reckoned she drove them on to stop herself thinking of what had happened. But this time at least she had chosen the easy route, the Black Bank, an easy half hour's walk. They would have to wait there, snug and warm together, at least two hours until the refugees arrived. Rest, that was all he craved, they would never make it to the meeting in Tim Healy's pub that night.
Billy was screening his eyes. Looking down into the snow flecked mist.

"I can't see a fucking thing" came his croaky voice, as Peter leaned close to his dark, bearded face.

"They're way below on the road. I'm going on. I'm dying for a kip and some grub."

Then he was on his feet, pulling his wind sheeter tight. And off into the mist. Thick mist now, and flurries of snow, wrapping him back into himself. Peter didn't mind walking, or climbing, once he got started, letting his mind drift away to the rhythm, into the refuge of dreams. In the mountains the only thing they really feared were the helicopters, which patrolled the edges of the last big free area, killing everything that moved. There were rumours that they would get shoulder launched rockets, but for now their only defence was to hide. So they had to walk fixed paths by day, and they dug foxholes, every hundred yards, fifty on slopes. Wet holes mostly, cut out of overhanging bog, or hacked out of the rock itself. Some were natural caves, and a few, like the Black Bank, were elaborate. Most days they saw the choppers and ran immediately for cover, for the big metal killers could sniff them out, especially in good weather. They had got Sonny and Macker McDonagh. They would sniff around awhile, then go away, for they dare not land, or leave their armour plated machines. Peter knew exactly where each hole was, he had to know, and he caught himself often, increasing his pace between them. Without foxholes you could not move in good weather by day.

Peter came down under the clouds, and down to the last ridge. He crouched there, scanning the pass. He couldn't see the refugees, away back, but the pass itself was certainly deserted. Just the two rocky outcrops, the gushing stream, and the winding road between. Of course there could have been a thousand troops lying in the bracken, but he would almost certainly spot them from above. Peter was grinning, under that first pile of rocks lay the Black Bank, dry and warm and room to sleep twenty. Perhaps the best appointed foxhole in the west! The main entrance ran from the small field of stunted bracken and gorse just below him. The second came from the stream, but you had to get soaked to get into it. The third was an emergency exit. He jogged down the last slope, wincing as his sack straps cut into his sore back. Then in among the thorns to the tunnel door. He didn't even want food. Just to collapse into a bed of dry heather. He began the long crawl, better than the freezing stream, and he could see light ahead quite soon, Max must have lit the lantern in the front cave. The passage branched, the other leading to the gun nests and the detonation points for they had the road mined up for two miles below. One person on watch in the Black Bank could in theory stop an army on that road. He was nearly there. They had spent a long time enlarging these caves, and he was proud of them. It was their place, their section of wilderness, and no one else knew the location of their foxholes. Peter heard voices, felt the warm air coming up to him, then he was in the big cave, where Max, Bernie and Michael were sitting around, chatting, warming themselves, and waiting for the soup to cook.

"Howayus."

"Hello Peter."

"Hey listen I'm going to kip down. Will you wake me in time to eat something?"

He slung down his sack and threw himself after it, into the heather in a dark corner. The voices irritated him, then washed over him, as he fell quickly into a deep sleep.

"Of course they look genuine." Max was saying, "probably they are genuine, all I'm saying is this, what's to stop them picking up a crowd of refugees, and walking up the hill. We come out to meet them, then the bleedin choppers come over the ridge.."

"Just one thing," said Fergus, "we'd kill them first."

"Oh great. So we massacre the whole lot of them just to get a couple of infiltrators."

"Well, maybe we....."

"Listen to me, " Bernie was up on her feet, "I'm sure they are real refugees, just lost and desperate and lucky to get here so late on. But if we want to be sure it's just luck, give McCafferty a buzz. If there's vultures lurking over the hills they'll know all it."

"Fair enough, so hook up the big radio, they'll be listening in now."

"Well it's worth breaking silence to be sure."

Bernie got up and began connecting the radio to a lorry battery, while Max made out the request in code. McCafferty's group were over the mountain, their neighbours, controlling the next section of wilderness. The reply, when it came, told them that nothing stirred. Max let out a deep breath.

"Right, get all your things ready now. Just empty sacks. We turn them back, then we go straight on, maybe we'll catch the end of that meeting. Okay who's staying here?"

"Me" said Billy, "me and Michael it's our turn."

"Peter, wake up, wake up."

He felt himself being shaken. Heaved himself reluctantly to his knees. People were milling around him, cleaning, stacking, unpacking.

"Here's your soup then," it was Seamus.

"Oh thanks, fair play to you."

The clouds had parted, and a think cold sun shone down from the top of the pass. William Barton turned, yet again and shouted, waving his long stick.

"Come on you slackers. This is the top here."

He waited a minute, watching the dishevelled, bent figures, shuffling closer. Hearing the creak, creak of the handcart. Then he turned again. For a moment he didn't see her.

Then he saw something else. As if she had materialised out of thin air...A woman, standing not five yards away just off the road in the heather. Bulky in green and brown waterproofs, brown face, fair hair flying. And a rifle pointed straight at him!

"Stop right there. This road is closed" shouted Max. A cold angry voice.

Barton's mouth dropped open. Then he collected himself. It was only a woman. He would move close, grab the gun if he had to. He smiled, a winning smile. Took a step forward.

Max jerked her head and the others stood up. William Barton looked around, and behind, dropped his heavy stick.

"Turn back now the way you came. Or you die here."

"We are refugees, from the Free" he shouted, "You cannot refuse us entry."

Max groaned, it was becoming a horrible melodrama. Two older women had rushed forward to join the big man.

"Please please let us through!" one was wailing.

"We have come so far. They are killing us back there."

"You are much too late" Max shouted, "There is no food, no more room here. Anyone can tell you this. The road is closed, you are crazy to follow this foolish man. Turn back. Go back now!"

"But where, where can we go?"

"Go north. Go north and west if you live."

"No way!" Barton shouted, fists clenched, "We're going through. You can't shoot us." And he took another step forward.

In one movement Max crouched, cocked her rifle and swung it to her shoulder.

"Die now or later. It's the same to me."

Barton took two steps back, suddenly convinced, his face paling as raw fear clawed at his guts. Behind him the two ragged women were kneeling, weeping and wringing their hands, while the rest seemed to be crashing out all over the road. An older man had come forward, and pushed Barton roughly back, shouting at him. And a small thin girl had walked past all of them, right up to Max. She glanced down, a cute triangular face, teeth chattering.

"I'm Susan" she said, "Can I come with you?"

Max shook her head, replied quietly.

"We're going over the mountain" she cocked her head up, "You can't come with us."

But the child was nodding brightly.

"I can climb up...Anyway I don't like this old road it hurts my feet."

Max sighed, she hated this. The older man was coming forward to parlay. Shuffling, head bowed, would he touch is forelock?

He apologised for William Barton, he wanted to know the best way north. Where could they hide? Where could they camp?

Max told him..the whole valley was a death trap. The gunships would destroy them, and enjoy doing it, further back the soldiers would do the same. The man glanced frowning at the clouds gathering above them. They would have to leave their cart and hide in the bushes and ditches till dark. Then go back, twelve miles, and turn north, twenty miles or so. There the country was subdued and they might just get into a work camp. The man had pulled out a tattered map and was holding it down, flapping, on the road. The child had crept behind Max, out of the wind.

"Hurry up Max!" It was Bernie coming up.

"You better all go now, it's dangerous standing round here."

"Wait wait" the man was pleading. "So we can't come to the west, could we pass through? Listen we have food left for three days."

Max groaned again, she really hated this, and the child snuggling up to her bum.

"Come in and go out. What's the point? They'd turn you back up the road anyway."

But the man's skinny finger was still jabbing at the map.

"Can we turn north here, over the hills, and go on north here?"

Max looked down blankly at the scabby bald head. She knew he had hit on their only possible plan. Then she glanced back at the women, huddled round the handcart or lying on the tarmac.

"It's a four hour climb across, for you, seven or eight hours. If they could go that far at all?"

"Yes, yes we can do it. We can do it if you show us the way."

"We're going that way" she said, then shouted "They want to go north to Tim Healy's and on out north. Will we take them?"

Heads appeared from the sheltering heather.

"Okay with me."

"Why not if they can walk."

"You can take the blame Max."

"Okay you're coming with us" Max shouted, "bring that cart up here and unload it. Now I want two of you with each one of us. We'll carry some of your gear and you'll have to walk fast or we'll leave you. You, what's your name?"

"Er, Willie Barton."

"You come with me I want to keep an eye on you."

"Me too." It was the child, hanging out of her coat.

"You better say with your folks" said Max, but the child shook her head solemnly.

"No parents?..Okay let's go..We want everyone well spread out. Leave at one minute intervals."

Max took the girl's hand, slung her rifle, and set off immediately. William Barton picked up his stick to follow.

"Put that stick down!" she hissed, "and walk ten yards behind me." Then she shouted, "see you later gang. Don't be telling any secrets now."

Max took off at a brisk pace, but the child, Susan, kept up well, talking and shivering non stop. After a while they stopped and crouched, so that the little girl could pull a woolly out of the almost empty sack.

"What's Tim Healy's Max?"

"Tim Healy's is a pub, a big warm pub and a farm, where we can eat and sleep and meet our friends."

She motioned Barton to wait, as she pulled the jumper over Susan's head. It came down to her knees. She rolled up the long sleeves and hugged her and went on.

"That man is funny."

"I don't like him" said Max.

"He wasn't with us before, he only came with us after the bad soldiers chased us the last time."

But Max wasn't listening, drifting into her own thoughts. The child put her in mind of Tommy, her own son, and Barney. Were they alive? Somewhere? Or dead, like this girl's folks, like Macker, like Sonny, like Paidin, like Maggie like...Oh fuck, like Josie, like Brian....

"An he has this funny radio he talks to at night."

Max didn't hear, she was pushing down a lump in her throat. then the words filtered through.

"What radio?"

"I'm after tellin you, he talks to it, I seen him."

"And it talks back?"

"It makes noises."

"Are you sure?" Max was gripping her shoulders, "Where does he keep it then?"

Susan glanced back down the slope at William approaching.

"In his coat." she said.

"I was right then. He must be one of them."

"One of who Max?"

"Um, one of the bad soldiers in disguise, some to spy on us."

"He's one of them alright" she said.

Max wondered what to do. Order him to strip and search him? Shoot him? In front of the child? No, she would watch him closely. Catch him in the act if it was true.

"We'll see about him later" she said, and pressed on.

Below them the guerrillas and refugees were stretched out, at intervals, in a long straggly line up the mountain. Sheep, they called the refugees in their radio talk, and like sheep they followed. Max scanned the horizon carefully when they reached the first ridge. Still no choppers. But they always patrolled this valley. Luck? Or because of the weather? Or because of William Barton's radio? Strange indeed if these people owed him their lives! But maybe Susan was wrong. She would have the man searched and questioned later. When night fell they would be safe. The evening skies had cleared, briefly, and it was colder if anything, but the bitter east wind was behind the silent mountain. She took the child's hand and climbed on into the dusk, glad now, after all, that she could help these people. She saw a pair of hoodies, grey backed mountain scavengers, break cover above them and wheel, cawing loudly, in a wide curve down the valley till they vanished in the dusk. Max felt her tense nervous exhaustion lift a little as the night slowly embraced her. The enemy would not come now.

Max was way ahead of the rest, climbing up and always up. The child had gone silent and dogged, then stumbling often, till Max was half lifting her. They were coming, still in shelter, near the top of the first pass. It was almost dark now. The clouds had thickened and were whipping just over their heads, but it was strangely calm, just a few flakes of snow beginning to fall, and the high keening of the wind over the top. There they would be exposed to its full blast, then down, and another long climb. Max wondered if the refugees could really make it. She was glancing back often at the dark figure of William Barton, who had come closer so as not to lose them. If he was a spy he must be armed, she thought. What if he shot her in the back, slipped away, and radioed in their destination? No, that would be too stupid. What if he had radioed in already when she wasn't looking? They could be walking into a trap! Just then the snow came thicker, in a flurry, as Max half dragged the child up a boggy sheep hollow to the top.
"Tell you what, you get into the sack for a while."
Max kneeled, and Susan climbed into the big sack. She seemed weightless, just skin and bone. At first she was up, arms round her neck and chattering in her ear. but the wind came suddenly ferocious and bitter, and there was nothing to see but snow. So she curled right down into the rucksack, as Max plodded on. And very soon she slept.
Max leaned forward into the driven snow and kept up a steady pace, she would not be the first to show weakness. But she knew that unless it cleared the refugees would never make it that night. It might still be a shower, a shower in the valley could seem like a blizzard up here.
What if he had already radioed in? And what if there were more of them. Maybe that old man was in league? She looked back again at the dark

plodding figure, now fifty yards back, noticing that the snow was settling already in the heather. Then she was fumbling at her buttons with numb fingers, and pulling out the radio which hung, plastic wrapped, around her neck. She managed to press the blue button twice.

"Hullo little foxes this is vixen. What's the story?" She waited and repeated the request.

"Skyhawks at eighty seven. Slow and steady."

"Red grouse. Heavy weather. One person carried. Over."

"Bogtrotters at one oh one. Rested once."

"Listen it's bad up here. We'll have to hole up if it doesn't clear. B.P. and Shay, can you search that old man, and come up to me at sixty four. Repeat, B.P. and Shay, search the old man and come up to me at sixty four. Bunch the sheep. Over."

"What's wrong? Over" came Bernie.

"I can't say but don't delay."

"Okay, coming. Over."

"Making tracks. Over" said Peter.

Max stood there a minute longer, watching William Barton stumble closer in the swirling snow. Listening to the high howling of the wind in the rocks above. She saw him fall and slowly pick himself up. He didn't look dangerous, but they would search and interrogate him anyway, better take no chances...She finished buttoning her jacket and hood, and she turned again into the wind. Now it was William Barton who was walking into a trap.

Here the land was nearly flat, then gradually sloping up again. Max could read the land, but she had to pick her way carefully. The man behind her found himself, again and again, up to his knees in icy bog.

The driving snow became flurries, and the flurries scattered flakes, and soon the first stars appeared. The trailing clouds turned white, and revealed a bitter half moon, rising in the south. The white shrouded peaks appeared, one by one, around the great upland bog. Max took in the grand beauty of the night scene, but the straps cut into her shoulders and her hands and feet were lumps of ice. The sleeping child was not so light after all, and a new pain was stabbing in her side.

But it was not pain that made her walk slower and slower, as she turned and came to the foot of a steep rocky slope. She was letting William Barton catch her up. Bernie, Peter and Seamus were still far behind, and she was coming close to number sixty four, the Devil's door. She reached the foot of the rocky scree, hitched her sack into a less painful position, and started up. Fifty yards up the slope turned into a vertical cliff, but they were not going that far. Max stopped climbing, lowered her sack gently into the thin snow, unslung her rifle and sat on a rock. Barton stopped at the bottom, perplexed.

"Come on, there's a cave, we'll rest up here."

Max began hauling away a pile of rocks, revealing a small grey metal trap door. She lifted it open and disappeared down a ladder. A short passage led to a high triangular cave, between two gigantic boulders. She fumbled with frozen fingers, lit the oil lamp, and then a small pile of kindling wood, dry heather and bracken, in the corner. Then Barton's head appeared, his hair an arrangement of icicles.

"Come here and mind the fire" said Max, "I'll fetch the child."

"Where is she?" he said, crawling out of the passage. Max didn't answer. If he was a spy he was a stupid one, she thought. She went back out, taking her gun, and gazed down a minute over the silent silvery wasteland. But she couldn't spot the guerrillas and struggling refugees. Then she lifted the sack, and eased it through the narrow trap, closing it behind her. She could feel the welcoming heat, the kindling was blazing. The smoke went up between the boulders, and was gathered into a pipe, which came out far up the cliff. A safety measure against the air force, though they still rarely lit fires by day. In theory the gunships could locate exactly a source of heat, and call in the jets to bomb it. But only a very precise hit could harm them in these caves.

"That's enough, you can put on turf now" said Max.

William stood up, the big man, and hit his head on a rock.

"God damn and blast it" he said, holding his skull.

Susan was awake, sticking a sleepy head out of the sack.

"Where are we Max?"

Max had sat down on a rock, rifle across her knees, and was pulling off her inner gloves.

"This is a cave called the Devil's Door" she said. "We're going to rest here a bit, and then Bernie or Seamus will carry you for a while."

"Why is it called the Devil's Door?"

"Because the cliff above is called the Devil's heel, there's no devils here really."

Max got up, rubbing her stinging hands, to hang the kettle and tend the fire.

"How do you like the mountain life then Willy?"

"Terrible. I'm soaked. I'm frozen. I'm exhausted. I think I have frostbite in my feet."

"What CoOp are you out of anyway? In the city?"

"Yes."

"Which one then?"

"South West."

"Oh yeah? You like the Magnetics then I suppose?"

"...They're okay."

Max paused, then asked a ridiculous question.

"Did you see them winning in the football final last year?"

"Er, no, I missed that."

Max almost laughed out loud. The Magnetics were a rock band from South West CoOp. This was child's play, she thought, in fact a child had trapped William Barton. Max sat herself down to wait.

"What group were you working in then?" She couldn't resist it.

"Er..carpenter."

"What group but? I might know it."

"Just a carpenters group."

"You don't know the Woodcocks by any chance?"

William shook his head, but did not reply, he was sitting near the fire trying to pull his boots off. Max was smiling grimly. It was too easy. She had worked six months as an organiser in South West. Their carpenters group called themselves the Woodcocks. It had become a joke, a separate group of women carpenters had called themselves the Woodcunts. Barton's cover story was an even weaker joke.

"Susan can you come here? Get out of the bag. That's right."

The child obeyed. Big eyed and ridiculous in the huge woolly.

"What's wrong Max?"

"See in the corner there. There's sleeping bags. Now get in one of them and don't move out of there." Max hugged her briefly, "Go on, quickly now!"

She wondered again if Barton was armed. If he was a spy he must have a gun. She must assume then that he had. A shiver went down her spine, and then she was angry. Here was one of them in the flesh. Those arrogant butchers who had bombed the city off the map. Who had killed Macker and Josie and Brian and all the rest, and probably Tommy and Barney as well...

"How many of these places do you have?" Barton asked.

Max tried to hold back a wave of wild fury, rushing into her, like the heat coming back into her blood.

For answer she clicked the rifle ready to fire.

The man turned slowly to face her, realising at last what a fool he had been. Suddenly catching the tension, aware and afraid.

"Oh come off it girl, you're too suspicious."

She swung the heavy gun in line with his stomach where he sat not ten feet away.

"I want you to put your hands on your head and sit back against the wall there. Do it. I know you're a spy!"

"But that's crazy.."

"Do it now. Or die!"

Barton was afraid, but quite sure of himself. Now he must disarm and kill her, before this went any further. It was past time to get out anyway, and his mission was not a complete failure. He would disappear into the dark, and call for a chopper to pick him up in the morning.

He stood up. Hit his head on the roof for the second time. Bent down, head in hands and cursing. Staggered a step forwards.

Max sat still on the rock.

Then he dived forwards! Max was half taken in. But she jerked the gun up and fired immediately. A deafening roar.

Then William Barton landed ontop of her. Knocking her back. As she felt Max tried to turn, but her head hit the rock floor, and his weight followed her down...

Max had the impression that she was sinking deep into dark water. She kicked out for the surface, pulling Tommy behind her. She couldn't breathe. Struggling towards the light which flashed, in time to the banging in her head. Louder and brighter! She reached a solid rock wall, realised she had been swimming down! Again she kicked for the surface, hearing Tommy crying and groaning, climbing desperately as the pain came pounding, louder and louder in her head.Then she was through, teeth clenched, gasping air. She was lying on a rock floor. She opened one eye.

Beside her the child lay crying. Across the cave the big man lay, groaning and crying out, spitting red froth down his coat. Max moved her head, but the stabbing pain stopped her. Now she could see the gun, it was beside him, gleaming yellow in the lamplight on the wet rocky floor. She knew she must act at once, but her whole physical being longed to slip back into the painless world of dream.But the terrified child had seen her move, stopped crying and raised herself. She looked gravely into Max's face, saw the eyelids flicker, and held a bloody red cloth against her head.

"Susan" Max whispered, "Bring the gun over here."

The child started back, and stayed there staring.

"I'm okay Susan, I bumped my head. See the gun on the floor. Susan! Bring it here so the bad man doesn't get it....that's it! Pull it over here now."

Max managed to drag herself against the big table rock, and balanced the semi-automatic weapon across her knees. The child snuggled up to her. Crying again. And Max remained conscious, listening to the horrible death struggles of the man by the other wall. It went on, it seemed, for hours.

A few minutes later Bernie, Peter and Seamus arrived.

It took William Barton three hours to die. The bullets had struck him in mid air. Ripping through his stomach and out through his buttocks. There was little they could do for him, even if they had wanted to. Seamus took the child away, to join the others on the long trek across to Tim Healy's.

Max's head was badly cut, but her skull seemed intact. They washed her wounds, applied antiseptic and bandages, and put her to bed, with earplugs against the rending yells of the dying man.

Barton had at least escaped interrogation, but they searched him where he lay, holding in his guts with his hands, and they found his pistol and radio and a little notebook in code. And they plied him with questions nevertheless, offering him whisky in exchange for answers. Towards the end his pain eased, and he spoke readily, in a barely audible whisper, Bernie prompting him and Peter taking notes. Barton's mind wandered off, talking about his wife who had run away from him. Talking about his father who he said was a top brass in the army. He had blundered. Desperate for life he wanted to tell Bernie his whole life story, as if by explaining himself he would somehow be spared. He told them all he knew of the invaders plans, and Peter knew finally for sure, jotting down the words, that the Free were really doomed. There would be no enclave spared in the west. Their mountain watch was a farce. Barton told them what they already half knew but refused to believe. The new government was functioning. The new native army and police had been re-formed. Food for work schemes had taken root and diversified. The church was calling on the last rebels to submit. Property was being returned to old owners or claimed by the State. The army had now completed their sweeps across the north and the east and the whole of the south, and they had consolidated their gains.

"When will they attack here then?" Bernie had led the dying man to the inevitable question.

"Yesterday..they called me out..yesterday, should have gone then."
Peter felt his heart sink even further. Till now he had clung to a faith in desperate resistance. But now he found himself staring, along with his living corpse, into the bottomless pools of horror and despair.

"How?" Bernie had said, "How will they come, how and where will they attack us?"

"Free fire zone...for three weeks" the words bubbled out, "Whole place a free fire zone, big operation my dad..."
Those were nearly his last audible words. Bernie tried to get more, but he was entering his last audible worlds. Bernie tried to get more, but he was entering his last panic, moaning and crying.
Then William Barton's radio crackled.

"Come in BB9. Come in BB9. Come in BB9."
Barton recognised the sound,but he couldn't move.

"Please help me" he managed, dribbling blood. But Bernie and Peter didn't move.

Eventually the caller gave up, and after that Barton faded fast. Bubbling and puking a bit and chewing his lips. Ten minutes later the radio came on again. But he was already in a coma.

Peter took a sleeping bag, handed the notebook to Bernie, and lay down by the glowing ashes. He didn't speak because he was sure he would start crying. Everything, it seemed, was hopeless now.

Bernie began composing a message into code, industrious as ever. In truth she was too exhausted and shocked to feel anything.

"ALARM. According to captured spy we become a Free Fire Zone. For three weeks. Probably starting at dawn today. ALARM. Repeat and pass on with priority. Good information...Mountain Force 33, Skyhawks Group...REPEAT..."

She transmitted the message to Donal O'Meara at Tim Healy's dugout, and he passed it on to the chain that linked throughout the Free Enclave. It was the only early warning that anyone got.

Bernie hung the kettle and revived the fire, staring a long time into the licking flames. Peter was not asleep, she could hear him quietly sniffling to himself. But she held her silence. When she got up to check the prisoner an hour later she could not find a pulse. She roused Peter then, and they found a piece of rope and dragged the stinking body out. They pulled and rolled it about a hundred yards from the hatch, and began to cover it with rocks.

The moon had gone down, it was bitterly cold and still windy, with a few clouds still flying up over the peaks, blotting and revealing stars. They worked in darkness and silence. Then crawled back inside and shook Max awake.

Max pulled herself together quickly, though her head was splitting. Irritable and furious with herself, she had to fight to think and act clearly. She supped at a mug of tea, reading through Peter's notes and cursing loudly...So the air force would come into their own. It would be another slaughter. Every building was full of refugees. Where could they go?

"If that bastard was alive" said Peter, "I'd kill him again."

"Did he mention Tim Healy's?"

"No...We didn't ask him."

"Shit shit shit he knew we were going there. He could've radioed when he was walking behind me!"

"Then they wouldn't bomb it, if they knew he was with us."

Max snorted with disgust, and went for her radio.

"Think like them Bernie. They'll guess we got him. They'll have decoded your message by now anyway."

She pulled the radio out, raised the long aerial, and pressed the blue button.

"Little foxes wake up. Little foxes wake up. Little foxes wake up."
A long pause, then a weary voice.

"Bogtrotters sleeping. Fuck you Hitler!" It was Jerry.

"Did you get alarm? Where are you? Over."

"We brought them down. What do you think?"

"Listen he could have told our destination. Over."

"We're kipping down grouse. This won't be the first, we'll get warning."

"Don't be fucking stupid! That guy's Da was top notch army. Just get them out to first base now! Over."

"What about the sheep?" Jerry was waking up.

"Warn them and leave them. Take what you can. But quick. Over."

"Okay then grouse. See what I can do. Out."

"Was that wise?" said Peter. "They probably picked that up!"
Max shrugged her shoulders.

"They won't change their plans now, if they're coming today...C'mon let's get out of here."

"Where to? What the fuck can we do out there?" said Bernie.

"Meet the others. If they're not blitzed."

"I'll sleep here. I can't go on." Bernie's tone was final.
Max whirled around, then decided to hold her peace. She glanced then at Peter, his face red and haggard. There was a silence.

"I'll come along then" he said.

Max and Peter hugged Bernie goodbye, before crawling out. It was still dark, but the sky was lightening beyond the eastern ridge. Max was trying to control the needles of pain and dizziness, which surged in waves up her neck. She was still furious. She had fucked up and put them all in danger, she had let compassion come before military sense.Peter was following in her steps, half asleep and hardly able to keep up. By the time they reached the second pass a faint freezing dawn had broken. Max stopped, clapped her frozen hands, and waited for Peter to catch up. She wiped her watering eyes, stamped the frozen ground, and gazed down north and west...bare hills and dark valleys stretching all the way to the sea. She could make out Tim Healy's on the road below, the big houses, cottages and barns among the stunted trees. She thought she saw flecks of light, torches maybe, but couldn't be sure. She wiped her eyes again for a better view. The wide, bowl like valley fell away before her, in the iron grip of the frost. The silence was total.

She heard Peter panting, and his footsteps behind her. then she noticed a thin high whine...What was that?

"Jets!" Peter shouted, running past her. Over the edge. The next foxhole was thirty yards down the slope.

Max crouched. Frantically pulling off her gloves. Tugging out the radio. She saw about ten jets in line. Cruising in over the high pass.

"Air attack! Foxes to earth. Foxes to earth. Foxes to earth!"

She flicked the frequency.

"Everybody hide!" she screamed. Up and running herself. "Air attack NOW. Everybody hide."

Slithering into a bog cleft. Max tumbled over. Landing on her back on thick ice. Cracking her wounded head....

She felt the world tip slowly. Still yelling in the radio. Screaming to a crescendo. She saw a big jet pass not thirty feet above her. Its belly fat with bombs. Her head fell back. She saw people running with nowhere to run. She saw great explosions of flame. And she saw Susan, a tiny stick like girl. Running, her clothes and hair in flames....

Lying in that icy hole, Max heard the first explosions. she grit her teeth, Max the hard woman. She had not cried since they got Macker. But the bombs kept exploding inside of her. Grief and guilt and despair. Then she saw the child's face again. And the world tipped right up and she was falling. Falling and wailing and beating helplessly, at the solid ice and the icy black walls of the cleft.

Peter saw the whole thing. Lying in the mouth of foxhole number twelve. Boiling with futile powerless anger.

He had fired his gun madly as the heavy jets swept over him. Now he watched as they cruised. Almost lazily, up and down the valley. And behind them buildings exploded in huge balls of flame. Farms erupted in smithereens. Stands of trees burst into flame. Then the crashing explosions started to arrive.

Around and around, in wide, shallow circles. Picking off individual targets. Neutralising possible cover. Foreign planes, must be a carrier off the coast...The great explosions kept on coming.

So much for their hopes, he thought, that international pressure might deter a final assault. Of course not. Any government would do the same. For in their small way they had challenged the whole basis of capital and the nation State.

The great explosions kept coming. Cowboys. Out for the morning's sport. Peter just stared, overcome with horror. He saw the planes come back into formation, above the huge pall of rising smoke, saw them turn together and come screaming up the valley towards him. Then they flipped. Suddenly and together, bombing straight up, with a mighty thunderous roar. Straight up, dipping their wings, and catching the first high rays of the sun. A crowd of tiny gnats, disappearing between the clouds.

Peter felt his mouth, dry as sandpaper. Did they even realise? How could they now know?

"Murderers, murderers, murderers" he was muttering. It was hopeless. They would bomb the whole area for weeks, till every little town and fishing village, every house, every barn, every wood..every hideaway destroyed. And only then would the army move in...What could they do? There was nowhere left to run. Would they hide like rats in their caves, and come down when it was over to try and slip in among the survivors?

Peter watched, as the rising black smoke blanked out the whole valley. The people blown to bits or burned alive below him. He saw Max coming down the slope. Saw first that her mouth was bloody. Saw that she was wet and crying, more blood dribbling from her bandaged head. Neither one spoke. Peter moved aside, and she dragged herself into the little hole, handing him the radio.

A minute later Peter heard a faint noise on the cold breeze. Then he spotted a new line of dots, in the bright sky to the north east. He had the radio in his hands, and repeated a message on both frequencies.

"Here come the fucking helicopters. Hide well if you're alive!"

ten **barney**

"What do you call a cop on a bicycle?"
"What?"
"A pig on wheels?"
"A moving target."
"How do you stop a copper from drowning?"
"Take your foot off his head."
Barney's loud warm laughter echoed from his lookout post by the barred
window, around the concrete hut. There were twenty three of them left in
that hut. There were thirty huts in the internment camp. Barney had been
picked up, disguised as a local farmer, after his guerilla group had been
surrounded and wiped out. He had not yet been identified.

Barney had been a rock of inspiration, during the months they had spent
in that hut, where their only facilities were only one plastic bucket. They had
divided into five groups, and diverted themselves in every imaginable way,
doing press-ups and exercises, and classes of all sorts. They had by now an
escape route, out through the roof. They were in contact with six other huts,
by flicking coats in front of the window in morse code. They played games,

endlessly, and debated the achievements and mistakes of the past, the tactics of the army and the resistance. But everybody knew it was all a front. Beneath the camaraderie all knew that resistance was pointless and hopeless. Yet as Barney argued, if they were going to be murdered anyway they might as well fight back. In the last few days four of their number had been dragged out to be interrogated and shot.

Barney's laughter was nervous and forced, a fair imitation, as he watched and waited at the window. He could see the outline of the watch towers against the night sky, their searchlights playing back and forth, he could make out the first perimeter fence and hear the hungry dogs barking beyond. And behind further fences he could see the lit up administration building. He could see, if he craned his neck, the lighted windows of six other huts. Any minute now the escape attempt should begin!

It was a mad desperate plan, and in other circumstances Barney would have had nothing to do with it. He had organised big robberies and raids before, going back many years. But this was suicidal, they had no weapons, no backup, and apart from that he had no means of checking, double checking and vetting his team.

Barney strained his eyes. What had happened to Gus? He was somewhere out there, crawling in the grass, with a length of thin steel cable to two bricks. With that he was supposed to blow all the fuses, sabotage the main electric supply to the camp. That would be the signal for the desperate uprising to begin!

"Come on lads, you must know a few more jokes."

"Wait, wait, wait" said Barney, and everyone was crowding to the window.

"Sit down everyone. Act normal. There's a line of fucking lorries coming in!"

"Jeezus shite."

We've been rumbled."

"Maybe a coincidence."

"Fucking crap!"

"Shut up, shut up. Remember the walls have ears. We bluff it out. Okay?"

"They're here! There's a lorry load of filth outside. No, two!"

Shouts and running feet around the hut. The noises on the roof. Inside the men sat huddled together. Barney feigned sleep, curled under his filthy old coat. There was a rattle of keys. Then the double metal doors swung back open.

Four armed soldiers came in the door. Followed by a sergeant and a a ragged prisoner. Barney was peeping out. Oh shit, they had caught Gus Evans. Or had he been a spy all along?

"Right we've got you bastards now. First we want William Kenny, John Fields and Bernard Maguire. Stand up over here!"

Barney's heart jumped in terror as his name was called. Nobody moved. If he had a suicide pill he would have it then.

"That's Barney there. That's Willie and that's John" came the voice of Gus Evans.

Barney felt himself doubling up in agony, as a terrific blow hit him in the back. Then a boot connected to his head. He heard screaming and roaring. Then a short, then a long burst of sub machine gun fire. As he was dragged out struggling to the lorry outside.

the door opened and a black figure became visible
tell them to evacuate the city said Maggie
Barney noticed without surprise that her eye sockets were empty
tell them to evacuate the city quickly
he was trying to give the message but his tongue completely filled up his mouth
he was stumbling after Maggie
cupping his hands to his mouth to catch the blood
the next room was totally in flames shooting about the room in bright flashes
floorboards were curling back and falling down a long way
he was at the window pushing people out stupid people it was quite safe to jump
he was standing behind a barred window watching them burn alive twisting and screaming as they jumped in flames from the fourth floor windows
tell them to evacuate the city he said noticing his own hands were burning red and indigo
he began beating at the bodies
get up wake up wake up .... Wake up!

Barney opened his eyes but only one opened.

"Wake up, Barney wake up."

Mick Wilkinson was shaking him. His head cracked back against the concrete. His face was slapped.

"Did you talk, Barney wake up, fuck you did you talk?"

Barney lifted his hand and Mick let go. He fell crookedly against the wall. Tried to speak but his mouth jammed open. Mick's head moved and the grilled light blinded him. He turned his hand, pointed to his mouth, and

shook his head ever so lightly. Mick clenched his fists and let out a cheer.
Barney noticed that he was not breathing and tried to cough. But a wave of
agony shot pains and lights up his neck. He was waving his hand
desperately, trying to inhale blood.
Next thing air rushed into his lungs. McDermott had his head down and was
slapping his back.

Eventually the tapping stopped, then continued further away. Mick had been
scratching out the message on the concrete floor.
"Did you get that?" Mick was up, pacing the cell. Waving his arms and
talking non stop.
"There's a hundred new prisoners from the camps in block nine. They
say the army is pulling back, its all over, the war's over boys and they're
going home!..."
Neither Barney nor McDermott spoke, Barney because he couldn't, and
McDermott because he had nothing to say.
"It's finished, the war's over! Next thing they'll be letting people go.
That's it lads, that's me, that's my life! ... Fuck your Revolution I'm going to
be free!...."
Young Mick was leaning over Barney's body, and delivering an endless
monologue. Then appealing to McDermott, who sat, head in hands, in the
other corner of the tiny cell, grunting the odd time when Mick insisted on an
answer. Barney was excused any answer, his tongue was still swollen and
infected where he had bitten it off under torture. He just turned his face to
the sweating stone wall and tried to let his mind drift. It was ten days now
since the interrogation. McDermott had tended him, tearing his shirt to bind
his broken figures, his burned lips and testicles, carefully removing his
smashed teeth...Barney was recovering, though some of his ribs were
certainly broken, and his tongue and his fingers oozed pus. He felt he could
recover, without medical aid. But inside of him was a big blank hole, and he
knew that his spirit was broken.
Barney heard Mick getting excited, shouting and kicking at the rusty
metal door. But his mind was far away, seeking out the dark shores of
delirium. Despite resisting torture he knew he had given up. His
enthusiasm, his optimism, his energy were vanished forever. He had lost all
interest in the time games, the mind routines, the endless tapping of morse
messages, the body exercises, the patient garnering of inner strength and
collective will that passed for life in these bare tiny cells. He hardly even
bothered with the agonising crawl to piss in the overflowing bucket by the
wall...McDermott was the real hero. Just sitting there, impassive and
seemingly indestructible, humming old songs of death and exile...

Impossible to ignore. Barney heard loud screaming and struggling in the passage outside. Now both Mick and McDermott were kicking the door. In fact the whole block were joining in, yelling and banging together. Barney screwed his eyes shut, against the possibility that they might take him too. He knew full well that he could never resist them again. His trick had been to go berserk, throwing his strong body into a shrieking struggling fit, which became entirely real, transcending all pain and ending only in unconscious. But he couldn't do that again. He would talk, or be forced to write, as they all did sooner or later. Then they would kill him and some of his friends on these blocks.

The noise had died down, at length. but now footsteps echoed nearer and nearer again. The keys and the clang of the bolt sliding back. The sound all prisoners fear. Barney opened his one good terrified eye. Saw Mick crouched beside him, hugging his knees. Saw three riot clad soldiers through the opening door.

"Mick Lavarty."

"No no no no" Mick was screaming, as they put on handcuffs and herded him out.

"John McDermott."

McDermott rose immediately, threw back his long grey hair, and walked out.

"Good luck Mac" Barney whispered to himself, as the door slammed shut.

Barney sat still, for what he thought might be about three hours, examined for the millionth time every crack, every dimple, every little bump in the blank white walls and ceiling. He examined the unbreakable plastic panel with the dull white bulb behind it, which shone for twenty four hours a day, or a week, or a month...for he knew not night from day. Then he examined the little white grill, where a little stale air seeped out. After that he began to examine the floor.

Barney was not depressed. Nor was he happy. He was not impressed with this bright new soundproof cell. He was no longer surprised that they had not killed him, or concerned that he was being used in some strange experiment. He was a prisoner. He had been a prisoner before and he had always expected to be a prisoner again. When there was no hope left - he thought, and often said out loud - the only place for a sane person to be is here in the isolation cells.

Barney was watching the door, there was no window. In particular he was watching the hatch in that white painted steel door. When he got really very hungry he would watch the hatch for hours, or for days, he could no longer tell. He had been fed eighty nine times, he knew that from the eighty nine plastic plates stacked in the corner. That was a fact, every time a plate of cold beans and chips, and from that solid fact he could trace his life in this cell.

The first six plates he had not even noticed on the hatch. The first thing he remembered curled up and naked, crying softly and endlessly and coughing up a little blood on the floor of the bright white cell. He hadn't been crying because he couldn't help it. Nor was he crying because he had finally talked. He was crying because he was not yet dead. He must have nearly died, he should have, but his body was stronger than he thought. He had been lying there delirious for a time of six plates at least, some could have been taken back. Even then he could have escaped, if he had been able to resist drinking from the toilet...And then he had found plates, and ever so slowly things had become clear. The strange repeating nightmares had become less real than the fact that he was lying in a cell. A bright white brand new cell, with it's own flushing toilet, door, light, and air grill, and very little else...Except for the silence and even more remarkable fact that it wasn't cold. It must be high summer he had decided.

By about the fortieth plate, half way through his life, he had begun to walk. He had thought the rate of feeding might have increased. Sometimes he got two plates in what he thought might be a day. But things had got worse again, or so he supposed. Sometimes he was sure they had decided to let him die of hunger before the plate arrived. He was watching the hatch now. Perhaps it would open soon...Many times he had been quick enough to jump up and to shout questions at the screw and to try and see out. But it was a double hatch, a double door. Cleverly arranged so that when one hatch came up the other was already down. You could not see out. Or try to grab the screw's hand...Built by a sadist, Barney reckoned, he hadn't seen anyone during the entire eighty nine plates. Nor heard anyone, there must be a strict no talk policy...They never spoke, no matter how you yelled, or joked, or insulted them...The invisible bastards stayed silent. He could be imprisoned by aliens, if aliens could make cold chips and beans.

Barney spent a few hours or so staring vaguely at the hatch. Then he go up stiffly, and walked the three steps to the toilet. Kneeling down and drinking a little water from shaking fingers. Splashing a little on his hairy face. His body was recovering. But he was starving. He raised himself slowly, knocking a skinny knee, and pissed. Then he flushed the toilet, and stood there, a long time, watching the water become completely still. Then he began examining the walls again, for a very long time, or so he thought. He wasn't thinking much about anything at all.

Barney sat upright in the corner. His long bony arms around his knees.
His great shock of filthy grey hair greased back. Mad red eyes darting
desperately round the empty cell.

Now that they were going to kill him he wanted to live!

Some time. Some hours before at least, the hatch had slid up for the hundred
and forty first time. But instead of a plastic plate there stood a hard tray,
with a dinner of hot port chop, veg and steaming gravy, rice pudding and a
cup of coffee.

Barney was up, as he often was, to try and trick the screw into speaking. But
he was too shocked to speak. Then as he lifted the tray the second hatch slid
up. He was staring for the first time into a pair of brown eyes!

"Your number's up Maguire" said a voice as the hatch slammed shut.

"Wait, wait wait" Barney was shouting. But the man was gone.

He was halfway through the food before his dull brain really grasped the
screw's meaning. The only possible meaning. They were going to kill him!
Then he began to wake up from his timeless daze. The outside world, the
past, became real to him again.

He was up, pacing and banging. Full of rage and sorrow. He was cursing
and shouting, laughing and crying by turn. Acting out angry conversations
with former friends.

"You know what the buggers did?" shouted Josie from her grave. "They
bombed the whole city in a circle till the suburbs were in flames, then the
fuckers started bombing the centre where we'd all run"

"Kill a few for me" Max laughed grimly, "If you ever get the chance kill
one on my account."

"You're right!" Barney swirled around, "We're only good for killing now.
They beat me to death but I came back to life..to kill just one more time...But
how? he went silent, backing round the empty cell.

"How can I kill them all with paper plates?" he almost laughed.

"Jab em in the eyes" it was Macker, leaping up onto the toilet bowl, "Jab
em in the eyes, then go for their balls."

"Hang on kiddos" came a serious whisper, "Probably they'll just open the
door and shoot him. Who cares? It's a soundproof cell."

"So I hide behind the toilet" said Barney, and everybody laughed.

Barney sat between the toilet bowl and the corner. Gripping the hard plastic
tray between his knees. Staring endlessly at the door. The excitement was
wearing off, leaving him weak and shivering...They weren't coming. He half
wished that they would.

Total silence. Barney was waiting and watching the door.

He was starting to feel really depressed, like he used to years before. He was starting to think about Max, and getting more depressed.Barney was waiting. He knew he would start crying soon. Then he would rave and shout for a while and eventually he would sleep.Instead he began to feel angry again. But still he waited and watched the door.

A sound! Barney felt a flash of pure terror. He put his head down on his knees, dropping his long hair down in front of his eyes.Keys. Sure enough... A crack. A bolt slammed. A loud creak as the rusty door opened wide.

"Come out Maguire."

Barney didn't move. Trying to hide his shaking. Peeping, he could see two men in riot gear in the corridor. But they carried batons not guns.

"Get up out of that you bastard."

One of them was walking in. The other followed, hanging back. Barney affected a dog like whimper.

"Get up!" the man lifted his visor to see better. Then he raised his baton to strike. And swung down.

But Barney had leapt to his right. Slicing the tray up. Chopping full force, twice, into the guard's face. Wrenched the baton from his hand.

Then he was on the second guard, whacking him with lunatic strength with the iron tipped stick. He had him down. Pinned. Was wrenching his helmet off...

"Stop or I shoot!"

Two men in suits, Special Branch, were standing in the door. Others were behind him.The first guard was staggering out, holding his face.

"Do me that favour lads" said Barney. And he swung the baton down, hard as he could, on the guard's skull.

Barney listened to the choking, gurgling noises for a while, before he realised with a shock that he was making the sounds himself.Then a loud banging began in morse. Barney opened his eyes, but it was completely black, and his eyes were full of liquid. He closed them, still racking for breath, and found himself spinning down again.

This is McDermott speaking" came a strangled shout, "They are gassing me to death."

It was the banging roused Barney again, and he tried to get up. One arm moved and his body convulsed in a spasm. His hand and head hit wood. Angry, he banged at it, not feeling pain.

"Who's there? Get me out of here!" McDermott's voice choked off.

"My eyes are full of blood" Barney tried to say, but no sounds came, and he began banging again.

"Who's there? Are you in a box?"

A box. Drowning. Who am I? Barney. Barney in a box.

His mind cleared for a second, and the terrible pain surged back. He tried to tap morse...B. A. R. he got, then he was fading right away.

"Barney!...Use your back......Barney?..."

But Barney had forgotten who he was. Unconscious again, though his body still retched and scrabbled feebly. He was not even dreaming now, and without oxygen his heart soon stopped pumping the useless blood.

And very soon his brain closed down for good.

In the next box McDermott survived a few minutes longer.

eleven **the trap**

There I was stealing desperate glances up at the big clock. I couldn't help it, though I knew full well what time it was. I couldn't help hoping that more time had somehow slipped away. It was fifteen forty five, just fifteen minutes to be waiting on the break, but still more than three hours to go...My hands flew to the razor parts. Lifting them from the narrow conveyor belts, clicking them together, and dropping them on a third moving belt...Stretch, lift, click, drop...stretch, lift, click, drop...me hands shot out and back, automatic. I could feel the strain in me back, and in my feet. But that was nothing like the dull, gnawing pain I was always enduring growing like a bleedin tumour in me stomach. That endless devouring pain, always coming in the night, and now invading my days, making me dull and enduring. Making me pale and flabby....fat!

Then I just switched my train of thought. A good trick all right. The endless switchboard of time passing, and me fingers flew!

Things I must do. I must see Aine, I had to see her than night. Aine my contact and now my friend, without her I could never have survived under cover. I couldn't have got that little flat, or this work, or survived at all in this sprawling German city. Aine risked everything to help me, her kids, her house and her marriage to that genial German businessman. Now I had to go back to her, to get her advice, to borrow money. Shit! I had to stop taking those pain killers. They were making me too dopey to act.

Stretch, lift, click, drop...stretch, lift, click, drop...easy, but so fucking fast I have to concentrate all the time to keep up. This is the fastest machine, and they switched me here deliberate. For speaking back to the bleeding supervisor, the only man on the whole floor, and a stickler for discipline, you wouldn't believe it! The women have to be totally submissive. Turkish, Moroccan, Spanish, German, so full of hatred turned in on themselves and against each other. And against me. We're all fucked over but they're making me the victim. Don't tell me I'm bleedin paranoid now. I'm the only one who nobody speaks to, sitting dumb at the tea breaks, though I know right well some of them speak English. So I got into me own company, singing little songs and talking to myself. Three months here and no friends. That's amazing. Then they start to treat me like some kind of a freak, giggling behind me back and all. There is so much hate and fear in this place it's like a volcano. And we're all of us infected, its like a tiny version of the world...oppression and paranoia, the military economy, race hate and hysteria, all bottled up and ready to blow!

I glanced back up at the clock, noticing that I was after getting pretty fucking miserable. I had to clench my teeth back against the pain, it would often come on like this, rising to a climax by the time the hooter went off. Leaving me sweating and shivering through the tea break....Stretch, lift, click, drop.. I cast my thoughts into another circle. The passport, that was my biggest problem now. It had been a false English passport, in the name of Patrica Dolan. Had been. I had left it in my coat in the cloakroom, the Wednesday previous. One of these bitches had it, or that bastard supervisor. And I wasn't even worried at first, dopey, a false passport lost, and I couldn't ever get a new one. This was a vital spring in the trap. That's it, a vast trap, ten years slowly closing in on me, only I kept on jumping out and escaping. Next day I was supposed to see the factory doctor, in the dinner break. It's a crazy system, I'm supposed to be an illegal worker, but I still have to register in the health bureaucracy, and pay as well! And even when you have a card you still have to show your passport. Shit! there must be a way around it, Aine would know. It ws only that morning, when the medical registrar made my appointment, that I recognised the next piece of the trap. I couldn't cash my paycheck without showing my passport, and unless I cashed it that week it became invalid! I just had to see Aine. Put the cheque in her account, that was it!

When I let myself look at the clock it was fifteen fifty two, christ you'd swear they slowed it down. Stretch, fucking lift, ten hours a day. Two beads of sweat met up on my forehead and dribbled right down my nose. I used to work round the clock with the Free, I used to climb up and down mountains like a goat during the war...this work is not so bad, if it wasn't for the pain I'd laugh at it...The noise used to get to me at first. These razor machines only whistled and clanked, but there was another that screamed continuously like the living dead. I'm surprised they didn't put me on that machine! And there was another one which alternatively ground and screeched. There used to be lots more machines, now its cheaper to hire hand labour than to fix them. Strange enough. Eventually they'll end up back doin everything by hand, if the whole world isn't blown to pieces first...

When I got really bad I would groan and curse out loud. No one could hear me, and the pain was clawing up like a knife in me guts. I thought this time I would surely collapse, as I suppressed another wave of dizzy nausea. I tried to think of Aine and her kids, but the thoughts wouldn't come any more. I tried to think of good times at home, but all I could come up with was flashes of Barney lying dead. Funny it was Barney now, not Macker and all the others, who came back to haunt me. I got no news of course, but I knew gradually, then suddenly for certain that he was dead.
"Fucking shite, fucking christ."
There was no way I could do it now. Tomorrow perhaps. I had this beautiful plan to turn down the speed on the machine. The mechanics were simple, a locknut and beneath it a graded wheel, one among thousands of nuts and bolts. At the tea break our section turned off the machines ourselves...but I would do more! I had a 13mm spanner under my pink work coat. The supervisor wouldn't accuse me, simply because he wouldn't believe me able to do it. He thought I was a moron like himself. Only the mechanics could speed it up again, and they only came usually when the machines broke down.

To hell with it anyway. I switched my thoughts firmly onto a safe track. Back home to the good times, those few collectivised years that still seem to make it all worthwhile! I remember when Macker McDonagh came to us, that was before the takeovers, I was showing him around the Free Area. Such a clown that kid he had me in knots laughing. We were down in the new dinner house with the rest when there was an alarm, the cops had nicked a horse and cart and two young fellas with stolen goods on the edge of our area. I disremember the details, but I remember cycling, with Macker on the crossbar, loads of us, all going the same way like in a rushing parade. Defence groups with coloured scarves. Kids with sticks and catapults and rainbow hair. Walking and running in and out. We were about five bleeding thousand when we got to the police station, flags and banners appearing, dogs barking and us on our bikes, bells ringing, dodging about. Pushing police lines almost playfully out of our way, waving our flags in the sun and the wind...They had votes on whether we should smash the Station, when we were already smashing it up, and this amazing theatre group with megaphones and giant masks, leaping up on car roofs dressed as cops and soldiers. It was a panic all right, I wish I could remember the lines!...On that occasion they freed the kids, and the horse and cart to be sure, and there was no riot. But the year after that the cops were swept away completely...

I noticed that my nausea had gone, and then I remembered being an old woman, still assembling razors, but an old woman in an old deck chair. It's a dream I can never quite catch that I've often had...I'm sitting there drinking the spring sun into my old stiff bones, and all these little kids keep bringing me flowers, and then sitting in a circle and listening for me to speak, and ... that's it ... I'm telling them I was showing Macker round the first Free Area. Such a clown that kid he had me in knots laughing. We were .... That was it! It struck me like I'd been pinched awake. I had the whole feeling of really being an old woman, so stiff and short of breath and a bit confused, but happy with those children and drinking in the sun...But the point of the dream was that if I was old I had survived, nay I was honoured, and I was talking about the Free as if they had survived too! That's the kind of crappy wishful dream logic that really cheers me up. My nausea had gone completely, even my gut pains had receded almost away.

In fact I would do it! I would chance it..Fuck the old bastards, the humourless repressive...I had glanced up at the clock, it was fifteen fifty nine. Stretch, lift, click, drop,....Stretch, lift, click, drop....Stretch, lift, click, drop....The hooter sounded.

As I pressed the stop button my other hand went under my sleeve, then I had the ring spanner in my fat fist. I slipped the other end up my sleeve, then the hand came out, and I walked as usual to the back of the machine. Glancing round at the weary women, as they closed down the assemblies. Then I flicked the back switch and the big motor began running down. I squatted, reaching in, and slipped the spanner on the nut. It was almost out of reach and the nut was dead tight. The other machines were switching off, I tugged, but still my heavy arm couldn't move it. I got in two arms, fuck it, and it moved! A fraction then a full turn. I got at the dial underneath and turned it half way down. I had only to tighten the nut. I pulled. That must do it. One more pull...

The spanner slipped, and clanked down into the machine. I turned. The supervisor was standing behind watching me!

The man smiled, then let fly in what to me was a torrent of meaningless German. I got up and just stood there, like a kid after being caught in the act. He motioned me to follow him but I shook my head. He grabbed my arm, pulled me a few feet, but I pulled back...The women were stopping in a gang and gawking at us.

"Fuck off" I shouted, my language has gone to hell. "I'm going to drink my fucking tea!"

The supervisor stormed away, and I just followed the others numbly into the canteen as if nothing had happened. I sat down alone for a minute, trying to think. I couldn't get it clear in my head...

I would be fired, certainly, third warning...but worse, I had committed a crime. They would check up on me, fingerprints, photos. I would certainly be identified. I would be interrogated. Extradited as a terrorist to face military trial for murder. I would be tortured for every fact and name I knew!

At last I was wide awake and furious with the world and myself. I leapt to my feet. Knocking back the chair. I had to get out now!

Then I saw three men,the supervisor, the guard and the manager himself coming in through the canteen door. The whole queue went gradually silent, nudging and pointing, as I walked to meet them in the aisle. The manager, in person, in the canteen! This was well worth watching! Those women watched in glee and horror, to see their victim trapped. While the men were asserting authority. They would humiliate me. Hand me over to the security police. It had worked well before, thrilling and cowing the rest.

Maybe I was the only person there who saw the situation in terms of a fight to the death. I am a trained soldier after all...Three unarmed men. One overweight,the others spindly. I had a good chance if I wasn't sick. My eyes were flying about for weapons, as I balanced myself, breathing deep and leaning forward in my workboots.

They stopped. Two metres away. Just when I was going to attack. The supervisor's arm shot towards the door, and he began in a screeching shout, his face going red already...I hated him so much, this potent puppet strutting over the helpless women. Suddenly I was entirely calm, totally aware. I moved, all my fury and pain and frustration homing in on one point.

I stepped forward, smiling, and kicked him a vicious whack in the balls. In the same moment I danced back. Lifted a cup of steaming tea from a table. Threw it in the face of the oncoming guard. As his scream began I took another step, I hit him smack on the nose with the heel of my second hand. He crashed at my feet as I jumped sideways, I don't know how I managed to do it.

The manager was backing away, dithering. I should have run then. But my cold fury was still rising, as the entire canteen stood spellbound, maybe encouraging me, maybe enjoying the horror. For those moments I could feel no fear or pain.

I feinted to dart past the manager on his left. Then swung up sudden over his arms. Chopped with the side of my best hand. Exactly into his throat, smashing his Adam's apple into his windpipe. I found myself, for a split second, whirled right around. Gazing into the eyes of about three hundred horrified women, as the manager fell flat on his face.

"You must fight back" I shouted ludicrously at the blank faces. Then I turned, deliberate and cold blooded, and executed a knee drop on the back of the manager's neck. Snapping it cleanly. I was up then at last and running for the door. And waving my fists, as spontaneous laughter and cheering broke out at last behind me.

I was sitting, hunched and shaking in a corner seat, head hidden in hands as the train jolted along. I had been dead lucky. I had run straight out the factory gates. Flinging off my work coat and pulling on my woolly hat. Had run straight into the station, flashing my pass. Just caught a train and changed at the next stop.

Now I had time to react, shivering in a cold sweat and squeezing my clammy cheeks, trying desperately to think. They had video cameras in all the carriages, but Aine said none of them worked any more. I must ring Aine to warn her, that was it. They would raid her house as soon as they realised I have given the factory a false address. If not sooner. And very soon after that they would have my real address. Aine was smart and stubborn but she had the children to think of. How quick and efficient were they? I had to go home anyway for new clothes and what money I had. What little money. What after that?

I looked up, and a small child was staring across at me with big blue eyes, clutching at his mother's knee. I had it clear now, but as the train rattled on I could find no reason anymore to run. It was perfectly clear. I was running in diminishing circles, the last rat in the closing trap. Then I was whispering across at the staring child.

"Death train death train death train, rattling on."
Well dressed people looked the other way, as I shook and shivered and fought back tears. It was quite clear now. I had to kill myself. I would deny those bastards all their interrogations and tortures. I would wipe out forever all the names I knew. No possible reason to go on. Every reason to stop while I had the chance. End of the line...But I must ring Aine!
I was staring, transfixed by the pattern of the metal rivets in the floor. Then I

looked up again, decided, caught the child's eyes and tried to smile.

"Death train death train death train, rattling on."

"Hello Aine? This is Tricia."

"Yes..."

"Listen I'm really sorry, they're on to me. I killed the manager half an hour ago. They'll be coming for you any minute."

"What, where are you?"

"Doesn't matter, I just had to warn you goodbye."

"Wait wait where are you going I have.."

"It's no good Aine I'm finished. Get the kids out quick. Good luck and thank you, goodbye."

"Wait Trish I have....."

I hadn't planned for suicide before but now I was mad determined. As I entered and slammed the door of my eighth floor flat behind me. I wanted to do it alone. I was panting like a dog, I was pushing the wardrobe to block the door, and giving up half way. Then I was at the kitchen sink, swallowing all my pills. But soon bleeding nausea overcame me and I began spewing up. Cursing and puking. Rummaging in the drawer for a knife, breaking plates...

I got my knee on my arm. Eyes closed, biting my tongue. I began sawing my wrist with the bread knife. Crying out and shaking with pain and fury. At last a good spurt of blood. Like a tough bloody chicken! No way to cut the other wrist. Blood everywhere, but it would take too long. I would have to cut my throat, quick!

Then I heard a key in the lock.

I was up. Scrambling to open the window. Roaring like a mad animal.

"Wait Max it's Aine!"

"Don't jump!"

I glanced back, Squatting on the sill with my bloody knife. There was Aine all right. And two fair haired women, holding sub machine guns, half concealed in plastic bags.

"Fire and I go out anyway."

"Don't jump."

"We come to save you."

"It's true Max, they're from the Free."

"I don't believe you" I said, glancing out and down. I saw a suburban train, charging into a tunnel. I saw my own blood falling, a thin stream breaking into dizzy drops...

I glanced back, calmer. They didn't look like cops.

"Look" the blue eyed woman had put down her gun, and sent it sliding across the bloody lino, "keep that, woman, you can kill some bastards, or come with us, we need you Max!"

"Do...do you have a doctor?"

"Yes, yes, there are very many of us."

I had looked down again, then up, as a line of heavy black jets appeared and disappeared into the low clouds. I had really wanted to die. My body swayed.

"Come quick Max we can escape!"

But I was already crashing down onto the floor and sprawling towards the gun.

"Okay let's go then" I said.

the end

●

a new world

We live in a free world. At least, that's what we're told. But in this society, 'freedom' means freedom for the few at the expense of the many. Freedom for the bosses to close down factories and offices, and sac workers; freedom for the police to beat us up and frame us; freedom for newspaper owners to control what we read; freedom for politicians to make and break promises at will. Meanwhile we are 'free' to sell our labour, our bodies and our lives; in return we get a fraction of what we produce. And millions are 'free' to starve while food is stockpiled in the massive food mountains of Europe and North America. Freedom in this society is a sham. East and West, North and South, the vast majority of us get nothing except more exploitation, poverty and repression.

But this has not always been the case. There have been times when people have broke through to discover new ways of living and new worlds. Worlds where we have real control over our lives, worlds where the idea of 'community' is not just some wishful thinking. Of course, we are not taught this side of history at school: the boss class wants us to believe that this way of life is with us for ever. But the truth is very different. The enormous battles in Russia in 1917, for example, showed glimpses of the potential. Factories taken over and run by the workers with the products distributed on the basis of human need not profit. In Spain, in 1936, hundreds of thousands of working class people threw off the chains of bosses and bureaucrats, priests and politicians, and started to build a society based on liberty and equality. Both these revolutions were strangled at birth by those trying to ride to power on the back of mass movements. But whenever the struggle for real freedom has been suppressed, it has only broken out somewhere else: in Hungary in 1956, France in 1968, Portugal in 1974, Poland in 1981, South Africa in 1984. Even here in Britain we could feel the bosses starting to panic in 1984-5.

This book is not a great work of political theory. But it is an inspiring and uplifting read. Despite being a work of fiction, it does recreate the atmosphere of Petrograd in 1917, Barcelona in 1936, Cortonwood in 1984. It has a vision of real freedom: freedom from hunger, freedom from discrimination, freedom from poor housing, freedom from isolation, freedom from exploitation. Such a new world has nothing to do with politicians, or bureaucrats, or liberal do-gooders. This book shows that quite clearly. For real freedom can only be created by the vast majority of us who have no privilege and no power: the working class. Some may say that revolution is impossible. But what's really impossible is the continuation of the existing system: we have nothing to lose but our chains!

organise

A truly free society will only arise from our mass struggles against the bosses and their state. But such struggles do not emerge from thin air. They develop and grow over periods of time, battles half-won and lost on the shopfloor and in the community. Often these battles are sectionalised and separated, moderated and then diverted. But on occasion they burst through the barriers that divide us and reveal a unity that sends the bosses and politicians running for cover. If we want to help build towards such explosions, we have to be organised together: otherwise we remain weak and isolated. The best form of organisation is at the base, in the community and in the workplace. Across the country there are many such organisations, from Tenants' Associations to workplace groups. There are also three main revolutionary organisations whose politics are similar to those expressed in this book: the **Anarchist Communist Federation** (PO Box 125, Coventry, CV3 5QT), the **Class War Federation** (PO Box 499, Bristol BS99) and the **Direct Action Movement** (PO Box 106, Rotherham, South Yorkshire, S60 1NW). In addition there are many other active revolutionaries struggling against capitalism and the state. If you are interested in finding out more about these struggles, **Counter-Information** (Pigeonhole CI, c/o 11 Forth Street, Edinburgh) is an excellent source of news and information. Some other good publications are **Merseyside Anarchist** (PO Box 110, Liverpool L69 8DP), **The Red Menace** (BM Wild, London WC1N 3XX), and **Socialism From Below** (PO Box 20, Huddersfield). Finally, if you are interested in reading other revolutionary books, write to **AK Distribution** (3 Balmoral Place, Stirling, Scotland) or **Active Distribution** (BM Active, London WC1N 3XX).

attack international

We are a small group aiming to produce revolutionary propaganda that is both relevant and accessible. The Labour Party, the Green Party and the tiny Trotskyist sects can offer no real solutions to the problems that face us: from exploitation at work to poverty in the home, from pollution in the air to repression on the streets. The only real solution is revolution: overturning the existing social set-up and building a new world run not for profit but to satisfy our needs.

At the moment we have one book and two booklets available:

Breaking Free. A full-length cartoon book featuring the adventures of Tintin in his battles against the bosses. "There's no excuse for this outrage" was the comment of the Metropolitan Police. "Hilarious: give it your little niece or nephew." (*The Face*). Price £2.00.

The Spirit of Freedom. A booklet that sets out to explain what's going on in Ireland and why it's in our interests to get the troops out. "Strongly recommended to everyone." (*Yorkshire Miner*). Price £1.00.

Until All Are Free. The trial statement of an American political prisoner. "An eloquent exposition of working class revolt." (*Leeds Other Paper*). Price £0.50.

We have also produced 4 high quality glossy posters: send £2.00 for the set. We are currently working on other publications. If you want to keep in touch, send us some money, and we'll send them to you when they come out. We also have a collection of leaflets and posters: send a contribution if you want some. And, of course, we're always open to any donations, large or small.

●